Emma's
not-so-sweet
dilemma

This book is a work of fiction. Any references to historical events, real people, or real places are used fictitiously. Other names, characters, places, and events are the product of the author's imagination, and any resemblance to actual events or places or persons, living or dead, is entirely coincidental.

SIMON SPOTLIGHT
An imprint of Simon & Schuster Children's Publishing Division
1230 Avenue of the Americas, New York, New York 10020
First Simon Spotlight hardcover edition December 2014
Copyright © 2014 by Simon & Schuster, Inc. All rights reserved,
including the right of reproduction in whole or in part in any form.
SIMON SPOTLIGHT and colophon are registered
trademarks of Simon & Schuster, Inc.
Text by Elizabeth Doyle Carey
Chapter header illustrations by Laura Roode
For information about special discounts for bulk purchases, please contact
Simon & Schuster Special Sales at 1-866-506-1949 or business@simonandschuster.com.
Manufactured in the United States of America 1114 FFG
2 4 6 8 10 9 7 5 3 1
ISBN 978-1-4814-1867-6 (pbk)
ISBN 978-1-4814-1868-3 (hc)
ISBN 978-1-4814-1869-0 (eBook)
Library of Congress Catalog Card Number 2014950717

CUPCAKE DIARIES

Emma's
not-so-sweet
dilemma

by coco simon

Simon Spotlight

New York   London   Toronto   Sydney   New Delhi

CHAPTER 1

Baking Hazard

My alarm went off and I hit snooze, even though I was already more than half awake. The Cupcake Club was coming over pretty early this morning to work out the kinks in a new recipe we were creating for a holiday boutique we were participating in, and I was looking forward to it. I snuggled deep under my covers and wiggled my toes in their fluffy pink socks. But I dreaded getting out of bed, even though it was a Saturday. It had been so freezing cold for the past week that I'd been walking around like a mummy in layers and layers of clothes (sleeping in socks and long flannel pj's), and to leave my cocoon of blankets this morning would be unbearable.

But then I noticed something. I could smell!

I'd been suffering from a terrible cold for the past week, and my nose had been totally stuffed up. I couldn't even taste the cupcakes we made at our last Cupcake meeting, never mind smell them cooking. (Katie was raving about the aroma, and I felt totally left out!) But now my cold seemed to have subsided, and I could smell the pancakes my mom was making downstairs. Their scent floated under the crack in my door, across the room, and tickled my nose, like in a cartoon. Cold or no, I had to have them!

I braced myself, flopped back the covers, and launched out of bed. My dad insists on keeping the heat lower than most normal people would. ("Just put on a sweater!" he grumps when I'm sitting at my desk doing homework, my nose red and running from the cold.) But today I am already noticing it must be warmer outside, because when I opened my bedroom door, I didn't have the sensation that I was entering a walk-in freezer. This day just kept getting better and better!

Downstairs, my mom was listening to an author being interviewed on public radio while she bustled around the kitchen making breakfast. Besides pancakes there were hard-boiled eggs with sea salt, fruit salad, and fresh orange juice.

"Mama!" I squealed, using my baby name for her. "What's the occasion?"

"Good morning, sweetheart!" my mom said cheerily. She put down the pan she was drying with a dish towel. "The occasion is that it will break forty degrees today! It's summer!" she joked.

"Wow, maybe I'll go to the beach," I said, and we both laughed. "What's up for today? The girls are coming over in half an hour to bake. We're going to need the kitchen, please."

"Okay. Let's see. Dad's out. Matt should be home from practice any minute. Jake has a playdate at eleven. Sam is actually around today; he's working the night shift at the theater, because he's got to study for exams. So a busy morning but probably a quiet afternoon around here." She put a plate down in front of me. It had a steaming stack of chocolate chip pancakes on it that looked like ginormous chocolate chip cookies.

"Mmmm!" My mouth was watering. I sliced off a huge pat of butter and slathered it in between the pancakes, where it quickly melted and pooled. When I took my first bite, the saltiness of the butter and the sweetness of the pancake combined with the sharp chocolate, forming an ideal swirl in my mouth.

"Oh, Mom!" I moaned. "These are soooo good! Thank you for making them!"

My mom smiled. "Glad you like them."

"We should really do a chocolate chip pancake cupcake. I need to get Katie on it. She's so good at figuring out what you need to do to make something taste like something else. Sometimes you almost have to trick your mouth. It's cool how she knows what to do." I took a big swig of orange juice and returned to the pancake stack.

"What was that new holiday cupcake you were working on last week? That one sounded delicious," my mom said enthusiastically.

"Well, there were two, actually. One was a cherry cupcake with pistachio frosting, so it's red and green for Christmas—get it? The other was blue and white for Hanukkah. The blue frosting was peppermint and the white cake was vanilla. It's a great combo. Kind of like peppermint stick ice cream. I think we've got the Hanukkah one down, but we're going to be tinkering with the red and green one today. My nose was so stuffed up last week, I couldn't taste anything, so at this meeting I think I'll be more helpful." I inhaled deeply through my nose, and my mom smiled again.

"Back to normal?"

"Almost. Much better, anyway. It was such a drag being sick."

Just then my dad and Matt walked in.

"Awesome!" cried Matt, running to the stovetop where my mom had a tall stack of pancakes keeping warm. He reached his hands out to grab one off the top, but my mom was there in a flash.

"Not so fast, mister! Wash those hands first!"

The boys' hands are always supergross when they get home from practice, no matter what sport it is. And they play every sport. Lucky me.

Matt rolled his eyes and reluctantly went to the sink. "Can I have six, please, Mom?" he asked.

"Must've been a big practice!" My mom laughed.

"Wait, can you save a couple for the Cupcakers, please?" I asked.

"I have lots more batter, so don't worry," said my mom. "I'll make a few more and keep them warm in the oven, then I'll clear out, so you can have the kitchen all to yourselves."

"The Cupcake Club is meeting *here* today? Oh, great." Matt groaned, tucking into his pancake stack (with a fork this time). But he didn't look too upset about it. My friends are really cute and my BFF, Alexis Becker, has a major crush on Matt. They've

5

even had some mild date-y interaction, which for me is cool and annoying all at the same time.

"You know you love it when we're here," I teased.

"Not," said Matt.

"Well, you certainly love the free cupcake samples!"

"Yeah, but I take my life in my hands every time I try one!"

"Well, if you think we're such bad bakers, maybe you don't need to sample anything or hang around my cute friends this morning. Huh? How do you like that?"

"No need to get all huffy," said Matt.

I knew I'd backed him into a corner, so I decided for one final push. "Go ahead and apologize and maybe I'll reconsider."

Matt scoffed, but then after a pause he said, "I'm sorry you're such bad bakers."

"Matthew!" warned my mom, but she was laughing.

"Seriously? And you think I'm going to . . ."

"Stop, Em. I'm just kidding. I'm sorry. You are baking goddesses. The best in the universe, okay? Now just make sure to throw me a few free samples today. That's all. A growing boy's gotta eat."

"Yeah. A knuckle sandwich maybe," I muttered.

"Mom! Did you hear her? And you and Dad always think she's the innocent one around here!" protested Matt. He shook his head vehemently. "Always the victim. And we're always the bad guys."

"Well, you did start it!" I said.

"Hellooooo?" called someone from the mudroom, and Alexis Becker appeared. A huge grin spread across her face when she spotted Matt.

I glanced at Matt to see his reaction and annoyingly enough, his face had lit up too. He was psyched to see Alexis.

"Hey, Lexi," I said, bounding off my stool at the counter. "Come see my . . . new winter skirt. In my room. It's so cute. I made it in my home ec class. I might wear it to the holiday boutique."

Her smile faded a bit. "Okay . . . cool."

I didn't watch to see if she and Matt exchanged any looks of longing, because I would have puked.

We headed upstairs, and soon after, Katie Brown and Mia Velaz came up to meet us. I showed them my new skirt, and Mia, ever the fashionista (even with a homemade skirt to work with!) helped me put together three different looks with it. Since everyone had arrived, we popped down to the kitchen to get to work, with my mom's chocolate chip pancakes to energize us.

We chatted about how warm it was going to be outside for a change (sixty degrees, which is totally crazy for this time of year) while I gathered our supplies and Alexis busied herself with our ledger, where we kept track of our profits and expenses and plans. Katie laid out her idea book, which was battered and stained and laden with awesome recipes, and Mia pulled up photos of some inspirational cupcakes on her tablet.

"Okay, here's the key, girls!" Katie withdrew a little bag from her tote and opened it. Inside were a few ingredients. We clustered around while she showed us.

"Dried cherries, pistachios, cherry jam, and—drumroll, please!—pistachio pudding!"

"Okay!" I said enthusiastically. "So what do we do?"

Katie explained how the dried cherries and pistachios needed to be rough chopped, which means chopped really coarsely, and how we would be incorporating the pistachio pudding mix into our yellow cake cupcake recipe, along with some of the cherries. Then we'd swirl the cherry jam though a cream cheese frosting base and sprinkle the frosted cakes with the crushed pistachios. We all took a task and got to work, chatting as we chopped and mixed and measured.

Jake and Sam both arrived and passed through, looking for swabs of frosting on a spoon or a lick of batter, but we shooed them away, with Mia (too generous always!) promising to bring them samples when the cupcakes were ready.

"Hmph!" I said. "You spoil them."

"It's fun." Mia laughed, her dark eyes twinkling merrily. "They're so appreciative of our baking!"

The cupcakes were soon in the oven, and I couldn't stop taking big gulping whiffs of delicious air through my newly cleared nose. It was like I'd been at sea for months and could finally smell land again. The girls teased me, but I didn't mind. The cherry and pistachio cupcakes smelled wonderful. While we waited for them to come out, and then to cool, we made the frosting and brainstormed about our holiday shopping.

"Everything seems so expensive to me this year," said Katie, her brow furrowing anxiously. She was whipping up cream cheese frosting in the mixer as I chopped pistachios.

"I know," I agreed. "I was at the mall the other day because the boys had to go to the sporting goods store, and even the sneakers there . . . It seems like the prices have just jumped all of a sudden."

"Yeah, we need to make some money. Do you have any modeling jobs lined up, Em?" asked Alexis. (I model for a few local businesses, but mostly for a bridal store at the mall owned by a really nice lady named Mona.)

"Not at the moment," I said. "I'm hoping Mona will have something soon. I know there's a new line she's hoping to get, so maybe. . . . The extra money sure would help."

"I'm hoping we'll find some cute things at the holiday boutique," said Mia.

The boutique is an annual tradition. It's held in the basement of our local Y, and lots of vendors come from all around with beautiful, mostly handmade and one of a kind items that make great holiday gifts. Candles, potpourri, customized stationery, needlepoint canvases and yarn, hand-knit scarves and gloves, fabric coin purses, special chocolates, fudge, and more. We would be selling cupcakes this year at a table in the refreshments area on the opening Saturday of the fair. It was a pretty big honor to be asked to participate, and that's why we wanted our holiday-themed cupcakes to be special.

While we chatted about who was on our lists to buy holiday gifts for (my list had my brothers, my parents, Mona, and the Cupcakers, of course!), the cupcakes came out of the oven, and Mia turned them upside down on wire racks to cool. Meanwhile, Katie carefully tipped three or four drops of green food coloring into the cream cheese frosting, then mixed it until it came out a delicate green.

I set the bowl of chopped pistachios next to the icing, and we were ready to frost. Just then, the boys came swarming back though the kitchen.

"Yum! Mia! Can I have a cupcake now? Pretty pleeeeease?" begged Jake.

Mia crouched down, looking at him with sorrow, and said, "They're not ready yet, Jake! We're going to frost them, and then you can have a couple, okay?"

"One!" I said sternly.

"But we're going outside now, to play football . . . ," pressed Jake.

"I'll bring them out to you. Now, shoo! Be gone!" I whisked them out the back door before my co-clubbers had a chance to offer any more free food to them. I shut the back door hard and could hear the boys laughing outside. "Scoundrels!" I scoffed.

"You know you're lucky to have them, Em," said Mia, laughing.

"Yes, I would love to live with Matt," joked Alexis.

I rolled my eyes.

Katie said, "It's nice to have such good eaters around, anyway. When I bake at home, my mom might try a tiny bite, and even if she loves it, she doesn't have more. These guys go crazy for what we make."

"I guess," I said.

"Come on, they're not that bad," said Mia. "Remember the time Matt made those flyers for us on his computer?"

"Yeah," agreed Alexis. "And how he always picks hanging with us over the so-called popular girls?"

"And the time Sam drove us to the mall to get your bridesmaid dress . . ."

"Which Matt paid for!"

I put up my hands, giggling. "All right, all right. I surrender. They're not that bad. They're pretty good, actually."

We were all laughing.

"Now fork over some of them cupcakes, and I'll bring them out," I joked to Katie.

Smiling, she frosted six, and Mia sprinkled them

with the nuts. I put them on a plate and headed out the back door, calling, "Cupcakes! Come and get 'em!" to the boys.

But just as I rounded the corner, tragedy struck.

Tragedy in the form of a very large, very hard, very out-of-control football.

It hit me square in the nose, and I remember an instant shock and pain, and that's all.

CHAPTER 2

Sooner or Later

I came to on the sofa in the TV room, with everyone gathered anxiously around me. I wasn't sure where I was at first. People around me were speaking in hushed voices.

"Her eyes are open!"

"She's awake!"

"Okay, okay, shh. Shh, everyone." My mom sat forward and smoothed back my hair, looking at me carefully as she lifted a cold compress from my face.

"Oh no!" cried Jake.

I sat up quickly, but my mom pushed me back gently. "Stay put. Just rest."

"What happened? Ow!" I moaned. My face was throbbing, and it felt hot and kind of tight.

I reached up a hand to gingerly touch my nose. "This kills."

"Emmy! I'm so sorry! I threw it! It's all my fault!" Jake wailed, in floods of tears now.

"Stop crying!" Matt said sharply. "This isn't about you!" He looked scared himself.

Jake tried to calm down, but tears kept streaming down his cheeks and he hiccupped. He had obviously been crying hard for some time.

"How did I get here?" I asked, looking around. Everyone's face was superworried, especially the Cupcakers.

"You were coming out with the cupcakes, and we were having a contest to see who could throw the ball the hardest and Jake was just taking his turn. It hit you square on the bridge of your nose," said Sam. "I'm so sorry."

"Oh no!" I groaned. "Is it broken?"

"I don't think so," said my mom. With me having three brothers, she's seen a lot of injuries. "I'm more worried about you losing consciousness. We've got to go see the doctor and make sure it's not a concussion. I already have a call in to him."

"Wait, I blacked out?" I said. "I've never done that before."

"We carried you in," said Matt. "It was scary."

"Thanks. Sorry." I shrugged.

"We're not sure if you got knocked out or fainted from the pain. It makes a difference," said my mom.

"Why?" asked Katie.

My mom tipped her head to the side. "If she only fainted from the shock, then it's a normal reaction to a trauma. But if the ball knocked her out, she might have a concussion, which is when the brain has been traumatized by the hit. It can be mild or severe, but it has to be handled carefully. Emma will need to lie low for a little while."

"Is there a treatment for concussions?" asked Mia.

"Not really," said Sam. "It's such a bummer. We had three kids sidelined from my soccer team this year with concussions. One guy—it was his second, so he can't play contact sports ever again."

"Gosh," Alexis said breathlessly. "Someone needs to invent something to prevent this. . . ."

"Sensing a business opportunity, Lex?" I tried to joke, but it hurt to even smile, so I stopped. My nose started to tickle a little from the laughing.

"Oh, she's bleeding again!" said Sam.

My mom dabbed at my nose with a wet paper towel. I could see that it already had quite a bit of blood on it. Looking at the towel made me feel a little woozy. I can't deal with the sight of blood.

"Do you have a headache, sweetheart?" she asked.

"No, I have a nose ache," I said.

"Do you feel queasy?"

"Not really."

"Good," said my mom, patting my arm.

"Can I look in a mirror?" I asked.

"No," said everyone all at once. Then they laughed nervously, but I didn't.

"That bad, huh?" I asked.

The Cupcakers smiled supportively, but I caught Jake nodding before Matt spied him and quickly cuffed him on the back of his head. Then Jake started shaking his head.

"Oooh." I groaned. "Good thing I don't have any modeling jobs lined up. Hey, how were the cupcakes?" I asked.

"We didn't have the stomach to try them . . . ," explained Sam.

"I ate one! I thought it was delicious!" said Jake.

Mia smiled at him and gave him a sideways hug. "You're our best little customer, aren't you?"

He nodded, in heaven. "Can I have another?"

Mia laughed. "And an opportunist, too! Sure, come on, let's go get you another."

17

"Hey, wait up!" called Sam. "Feel better, Em," he said with a wink, and he headed into the kitchen.

Matt trailed behind them, and my mom went to call the doctor again. I was left with Alexis and Katie. "How bad is it?" I whispered, now kind of dreading seeing it.

"Oh, you know . . . ," said Katie vaguely.

Alexis set her lips in a grim line. "You're going to look awful for a few days. But then it will be fine. No permanent damage."

"Alexis!" said Katie, shocked at her bluntness.

"What?" said Alexis, huffy now. "It's true. Why should I lie to her?"

"Hey, no. It's fine. I wanted the truth," I said. "It's better to know. I'll see it, anyway, sooner or later, right?" I reached up to try to feel around, and I could definitely feel the swelling all across my face. "Ugh."

"Yeah, better if later," agreed Alexis. "Rather than sooner, I mean." She glanced guiltily at Katie, who just shook her head.

My mom came bustling back in. "Okay, the doctor can take a look at you if we head over now. Are you okay to try to sit up?"

I swung my legs over the side of the sofa and sat up tall, but I suddenly got a head rush, and things were a little spinny for a minute. I glanced at my mom, and her face was really worried, so I tried to pull it together for her sake, anyway. I took a deep breath.

"Okay," I said.

Soon I was up on my feet and walking a bit wobbly out to the car, the Cupcakers trailing behind.

"We'll just clean up here, then head out, so you can come home and rest," said Alexis from the door.

"And we'll walk Jake to his playdate," added Mia. My mom thanked her.

"No, feel free to stay. I won't be long." We were supposed to head to Scoops ice-cream shop for grilled cheese and milk shakes later. "We can go after."

Alexis grimaced. "I don't know if you're going to want to go out when you get back," she said, shrugging helplessly.

I sat down in the backseat of the minivan. "Oh boy," I said.

Alexis gave a sigh. "Just don't look in the mirror."

She was right.

On the way to the doctor's I couldn't face my reflection. I was worried if it looked really bad, I wouldn't want to get out of the car. The doctor was supernice, and he gave me all sorts of funny tests, asking me things like what the date was a week ago on Thursday and to do some simple puzzles and stuff, and he concluded that I did not have a concussion, which was my mom's main concern.

"The site of the impact is a factor," he told my mom. "And noses absorb a lot of impact. Two inches higher . . ." And then he shrugged. "One thing's for sure, Emma. Your brain should be grateful to your nose. It really took one on the chin today!" Then he laughed at his own bad joke.

I smiled. "I guess," I said. "But how bad is this nose going to look and for how long?" I tried not to whine, but I was worried.

He shook his head. "Hard to say. You'll probably reach maximum swelling through tomorrow, and then that will start to calm down, but don't be surprised when the black eyes appear tomorrow or the next day. Those can take a while to fade too."

"Oh great," I said sarcastically.

He looked at me sympathetically. "I know. It really is a drag, but it could have been a lot worse. Your nose didn't even break. You've been drinking your milk!"

He looked at his watch, and we all stood up.

Then he continued, "I'm very glad you don't have a concussion, Emma. I've had kids out of school for weeks because they'd get a migraine every time they looked at a white sheet of paper. And that meant while they were home, no TV, no computer, and no phone. Nothing to overstimulate or irritate the brain. Trust me, it's just awful. I hate to see it."

"I know. I'm glad I avoided that too."

"Just ice the nose a lot, drink tons of water, and take aspirin, and you'll be just fine."

We thanked him and headed our separate ways.

In the car, my mom said, "Well, that's a relief."

"I guess," I said, lowering the visor and flipping open the mirror. I took a deep breath through my mouth and braced myself.

And then I took one look at my bashed-up face and burst into tears. It was awful. I had a huge bump across the bridge of my nose, and the skin was broken and bloody, and a huge dark blue bruise was smeared across my nose, and even starting under my eyes. But what was worse was the swelling. I looked like an alien. The center of my face, including my nose and the area between my eyebrows, was so swollen that the space between the inside corners of my eyes had doubled.

"On no." I began to sob, which of course made my nose hurt more and my face look even uglier. "I'm not going to be able to leave the house for weeks!" I wailed.

My mom put her arm around me and hugged me tightly. "I think you're going to have to wear a hat and maybe some sunglasses for a few days," she whispered into my hair.

"More like for the rest of my life!" I whimpered.

CHAPTER 3

Smushed

That afternoon, I was lying on the couch with yet another ice pack on my nose when the phone rang. My mom picked it up in the kitchen, but I couldn't hear who she was speaking with. Then she came and peeked her head into the TV room, the phone clutched close to her chest. I think she thought I might be asleep, but I wasn't.

"Oh. It's Mona," she whispered. "Can you take it, or should I tell her you'll call her back?"

"I can take it," I said, sitting up. *Did you tell her?* I mouthed, and gestured at my nose. My mom shook her head, and I gave her a thumbs-up.

"Hi, Mona," I said into the phone, trying to sound bright and cheerful. I do love Mona, but I was really not feeling my very best at that exact moment.

"*Darling*! How *are* you?" Mona is a very dramatic speaker. A very dramatic person in general, actually. I had to smile when I heard her familiar, throaty voice.

"I'm . . . pretty good," I lied, crossing my fingers.

"Well, I have the most *divine* news," said Mona, using her favorite adjective. There was a dramatic pause, and then she announced, "Harry Rosner has finally agreed to let me carry his line. Can you stand it? *Harry Rosner* at The Special Day bridal salon!"

"Congratulations, Mona!" I said enthusiastically. I was genuinely happy for her; she'd been pursuing Rosner's very exclusive line for a year or more.

"Thank you. It's too, too *faboo*! So he'd like to come in later this week, and he'll have some bridesmaids samples, and I wondered if you might be free for a spell after school one day?"

"Oh . . . I . . ."Yikes! I wanted the job, I needed the money, and I wanted to help Mona out. But my *nose*! Could I really show up to model looking like this? I had to tell her the truth. "Well, Mona, I'd love to do it. There's just one little problem. . . ." I explained about my nose.

"Oh, darling, don't be ridiculous!" she said emphatically. "You're divine, nose or no nose. Harry Rosner can see past that, anyway. He's a professional.

We're just looking at fit and drape. It has absolutely nothing to do with noses!" she said.

I wasn't so sure about that. I'd heard Harry Rosner was a perfectionist, handpicking every account that carried his work, and even handpicking many of the models.

"Well . . ." I stalled.

"Just say yes, darling. We'll cross the nose bridge when we come to it. Thursday? Friday?" she offered.

As much as I wanted the extra day for healing, I had to bake on Friday for the holiday boutique. "Um, let's say Thursday, then, if you really think it won't matter?"

"Darling, you'll look *divine*. See you then. Thanks so much. Big kiss!" And she made some kissy sounds and hung up.

I clicked off the phone and breathed a huge sigh of dread. "Oh boy," I whispered. I took a selfie with my phone, so everyone could see how this injury had progressed, then I texted it and the news to the Cupcakers, asking for any advice. With Mia's mom a stylist, and Katie's mom a dentist, I figured someone, somewhere might have some advice for me.

Sure enough, Mia invited us all over the next day and promised that her mother would be on hand with advice. Phew. At least it was a start! I hoped I would already be on the mend by then.

But boy was I wrong!

The first thing I did when I woke up on Sunday was race to the mirror over my dresser to inspect my face.

"Noooo!" I wailed. Even though the doctor said it was possible, it was worse today than yesterday. The bridge of my nose was a deep reddish purple, and massive blue circles had appeared under my eyes, like Jake had colored my face with his crayons. I looked like a colorful raccoon!

I spent the morning doing my homework and icing my face, debating whether I could even leave the house. Finally, my mom pointed out that since there was no way I was staying home from school on Monday, I might as well get used to being out in the world, and I decided I'd go to Mia's after all.

I arrived at Mia's after lunch, and the other Cupcakers were there; had been there, it seemed, for a little while. When I walked into the kitchen, they were hiding something behind them. Alexis's eyes twinkled, and Katie was obviously trying to stifle a giggle.

"What?" I said, a dumb smile on my face. I could tell there was a joke about to be revealed.

Then Katie and Alexis stepped apart, and Mia called, "Tadaaaaa!" I saw a platter of cupcakes behind them. Bacon and caramel cupcakes, in fact. My favorite kind!

"Oh, guys! That is so nice! My favorite!" I crossed the kitchen to the platter, but everyone was giggling now.

"What?" I asked suspiciously. "Are they poisoned?"

"Just look closely!" Katie blurted, so I did.

Every one of the cupcakes was smushed a little, or dented. Just . . . imperfect. Like, we would have rejected any one of them if they were for a client.

"Get it?" Alexis laughed.

"Ummm . . . they were all dropped?" I offered.

"No! They're all a little smushed on the outside, but still perfect on the inside. Like *you*!" said Alexis, giggling.

"Ohhhh . . . ," I said, in an *I get it* tone of voice. But I couldn't giggle back. It just wasn't funny, really. I mean, I know *they* thought it was funny and clever, or whatever, but . . . they weren't the ones with dented faces.

I glanced at Mia and saw her looking at me

sympathetically. Then she said briskly, "Okay. Not funny. Sorry about that, Em. The joke fell flat. We thought it was sending you a positive message, but . . . maybe it's a little too soon. Never mind! Let's just eat the cupcakes and forget about the whole mess, okay?" Mia reached over and grabbed me in a hug. "Sorry," she whispered into my hair. I smiled at her gratefully.

"Thanks," I said. "Anyway, thanks, all of you, for the cupcakes. It really was thoughtful."

Alexis and Katie nodded quietly. "Sorry," they both said.

I waved it off. "Don't be silly. I'm just being oversensitive."

Mrs. Valdes walked in, then, with warm greetings for me. She hugged me, then held me at arm's length and studied my face. "Oh, *mija*, don't worry! With a little concealer, no one will see it at all."

"Oh, I almost forgot!" Katie said, lifting a tiny shopping bag from the side counter. "These are some holistic remedies for swelling and bruising, from my mom. It's her new thing—holistic and herbal medicine. Anyway, it can't hurt, right?"

"Thanks, Katie!" I said, giving her a big hug.

We chatted with Mrs. Valdes while we ate our cupcakes, and then we headed up to her fancy and elaborate dressing table in the sitting area of her bedroom. The other girls sprawled on her bed and loveseat while I sat in the dressing table chair and Mrs. Valdes pulled up a little bench. She directed the magnifying light on me, and I winced at the brightness.

"Sorry! I know, it is so bright, but the good news for you is you have such gorgeous skin, it still looks great under this light! I, for one, should retire the bright bulb for something a little more flattering!"

I smiled, and she lightly took my chin in her hand and turned my head this way and that, nodding. Then she pulled out a handful of sticks and creams and tubes and got to work, very gently brushing cosmetics onto my nose, my under-eye area, and a little bit of my forehead, stopping occasionally to blend it in and then pull back and squint at me. Finally, she seemed satisfied with her work. She took a massive fluffy brush, dabbed a little powder on it, tap-tap-tapped it off, and after telling me to close my eyes, she dusted my face. (It all actually felt really good.) Then she said, "*Bueno*. Look in the mirror, *mi amor*."

And I looked.

I couldn't believe it! Aside from the swelling,

which only I and maybe my closest family and friends would even notice, there was no sign of the bruising whatsoever. I stood up and leaned on the dressing table to get a closer look in the mirror, turning my head from side to side.

"Wow!" I said breathessly. "Thank you!"

The other girls crowded around, inspecting me.

"That's amazing! Like magic!" cried Alexis.

Mrs. Valdes just smiled calmly and shrugged fake-modestly. "All in a days' work!" And we laughed.

"So what should I get at the drugstore, so I can do this at home?" I asked, getting down to business.

Mrs. Valdes said she would give me a few of her things, and when I protested, she waved me off, saying she gets free samples all the time. Then she went to her closet and took out a big plastic tub and laid it on the bed. It said SAMPLES across the top in hot pink marker. She lifted the lid, and we all gasped. Inside was every brand name cosmetic you could think of, all in their original box or package, all in sample sizes.

Mrs. Valdes laughed. "See? I can't get rid of them fast enough! I think they multiply while they sit in this box!"

"It's like Christmas!" said Katie, who doesn't even wear makeup.

"All these are *free* samples?" Alexis asked incredulously. "How can this be economical for these companies?"

We laughed, because Alexis will always look at the business angle of things. That's why she's CFO of the Cupcake Club.

"Go ahead, help yourselves," instructed Mrs. Valdes. "Just let me pull a few things I know Emma will need." And she sifted through the box, selecting a tiny powder compact, a set of mini–makeup brushes in a small Christmas-themed box ("Merry Christmas!" she said, handing them to me), and a little tube of concealer and a jar of foundation.

"Wow, thank you so much, Mrs. Valdes," I said gratefully.

"My pleasure, my dear. Let's quickly go over how to apply it all. I'll write it down for you, even."

"Great!" I said.

I knew I was lucky to have such great friends, but I was even luckier that they had such great moms!

CHAPTER 4

School Daze

After our fabulous cosmetics interlude, we decided we'd better go downstairs for another cupcake, smushed or not. At the table, I opened the bag from Katie's mom to see what was inside. There was a white note card with Mrs. Brown's small, neat handwriting that listed what was there and what to do with it. It said:

Arnica cream: apply in the morning and at bedtime, a light layer over all areas of bruising.

Parsley: make a paste by pulverizing the leaves and adding a tiny bit of water, then apply thickly over the bruised area and allow to sit for fifteen minutes.

Tea bag: steep the tea for one minute in hot tap water, then remove bag, squeeze out excess water, and apply to bruise, allowing it to sit on area for fifteen minutes.

I looked back into the bag, and there was a tube of arnica cream, a bunch of parsley in a plastic produce bag, and a small box of organic black tea bags.

"Wow, Katie, this is so awesome! Thank you! I'll e-mail your mom later to say thanks. This is so very thoughtful."

Katie rolled her eyes like it was a little embarrassing. "Who knows if it will work or not."

"It's totally worth a try," I said. "At least I'll feel like I'm doing something rather than sitting around feeling sorry for myself."

We wrapped up the afternoon by reviewing our holiday shopping lists together. I knew I wanted to get my mom a pancake skillet and/or a new book or gift card from the bookstore at the mall. I wanted to get my dad a coach's whistle and a new clipboard, because he lost his at a soccer game recently and had been kind of looking for it ever since. For my brothers, I figured I'd get them each something sporty at the sporting goods store, like socks, or if I couldn't find anything there, then maybe an iTunes gift card. It seemed a little lame and maybe not that imaginative, so it was hard to get excited about the boys' gifts. Also, it would all be kind of expensive.

Mia went over what she was getting for her parents and her stepfather, Eddie, and her stepbrother, Dan. Then Alexis shared her ideas for her parents and admitted that she was totally stumped when it came to her older sister, Dylan, who we all knew was superpicky and hard to please. When it came to Katie's turn, she said, "Well, I only have my mom, so it's pretty easy. And I like to do a stocking for her." She explained what she was planning to put in it this year. It was all very thoughtful, and it made me kind of wince at my lack of originality, and also because I sometimes feel a little bad for Katie that she has such a small family. I mean, half the time I'd really be happier without my brothers around, but after a while it would get lonely and boring.

"Oh, also, I was thinking I might do a stocking for Mr. Green." Katie shrugged casually, as if it was no big deal. But it kind of was. Her mom had been dating a math teacher from our school for a while, and we were all very supportive of it, even if it was a little awkward for Katie. "And maybe one for his daughter, Emily, too."

"Hey, we're shopping for one another this year too, right?" Alexis said brightly.

Mia nodded. "I am, but only 'cause I think it's

fun. No one needs to get me anything." Mia is a really good shopper, always finding unique things at great prices.

"Oh, please! Like we'd forget about you for the holidays!" I joked.

"I'm just saying . . ." Mia shrugged.

"And what about . . . um, is anyone buying anything for anyone else?" asked Alexis a little too casually, looking intently at her fingernails like they suddenly contained the key to the universe.

Mia said, "Well, I'll get something for Ava, of course." Ava is her best friend from when she lived full-time in the city. We all know her and have become friends with her too, through Mia.

Katie said shyly, "I was thinking of getting something for George. I don't have as many people to buy for as you all do, so . . ." She smiled a shy smile and folded her arms.

"You go, girl!" said Mia.

"So someone *is* buying for a boy!" said Alexis with a big grin.

I had to crack up. "Did you have anyone in mind, Lexi?" I teased.

She looked up innocently. "What? Me? Oh, well. I mean. I just wondered if anyone was. You know . . ." Her voice trailed off.

"Matt would love anything sporty," I said, "if that is useful information to anyone here." I purposely looked away from Alexis.

"Actually, I was thinking it would be fun to get something for Jake," Mia said. "It's fun to buy for kids at holiday time, and he's kind of the only kid I really know."

"Hey, that reminds me!" said Katie, standing so she could pull something from her back pocket. She unfolded a flyer and put it on the kitchen table. "We should donate to this!"

It was a notice for a children's holiday party to be held at the hospital this Sunday, with refreshments, games and prizes, and a visit from Santa, who would have gifts for all the kids.

"Cute!" I agreed. "Let's do it!"

Alexis was squinting at the flyer, which had a contact name at the bottom and an e-mail address. "I'll get in touch with this Kathy Dwyer to see if she'd like us to donate cupcakes. They'll need to be nut free, I'm sure. And festive. So we can do the Hanukkah ones we're doing for the holiday boutique, but we'll need to come up with another recipe for Christmas."

"Sounds good," I said, and smiled, which kind of made my face feel like it was going to crack and fall off. "Hey, do you think your mom would mind if I washed this off now?" I asked Mia.

"No," she said, laughing. "Can't stand it?"

I shook my head. "It itches after a while."

"Occupational hazard for a model!" she teased.

"I know. But I'd also love to get some of these tea bags on my face. No time like the present!" I said, thinking of my upcoming date with Mona.

When I got home from Mia's, I did the parsley paste and later went to bed with a thick layer of arnica cream on my face. It kind of stung at first, but I told myself that meant it was working, and eventually I did fall asleep.

And lo and behold, it worked!

When I woke up the next day, I rushed to my mirror again (a new ritual), and the bruising was visibly better! I mean, I still looked like a freak, like the victim of a boxing match with the heavyweight champion of the world. But even Jake said at break-fast, "Emmy, your black eyes are turning greenish!" and I had to thank him. That was a compliment in our house these days, after all.

I was still dreading going to school for the first time since the Big Hit (as I had come to think of it). I knew everyone would be trying to say funny stuff all day like, "I'd hate to see the other guy" and "Did you get the license plate of the bus that hit you?" I braced myself to just smile and let it roll off my back, knowing my reaction would all depend on who said it. I braided my hair, pulled one of Sam's newer baseball hats onto my head, and used some of Mrs. Valdes's miracle cream to lighten up the bruising. I looked okay but still not good. Sighing, I trudged off to school.

Needless to say, the day was filled with casual cruelty in the form of people trying to be funny, but other people were surprisingly nice. A quiet girl in my math class named Ann Roberts patted my shoulder and told me that the same thing had happened to her a few years ago, and it goes away pretty fast. One of the lunch ladies gave me extra dessert. So it all evened out in the end.

It wasn't until my last class of the day that some-one's arrow really hit the mark. Naturally, it was Olivia Allen who launched it. She was whispering with a friend as I was walking down the hall, and they both immediately stopped talking when I got close, exchanging knowing looks. Shortly after, I felt a nudge on my arm, and it was a note, from Olivia.

I opened it and inside it said: *Dr. Kaminow. City Hospital. He's the best.*

I furrowed my brow, trying to figure out what it meant. Olivia made a fake sad face, trying to look sympathetic. And then as she walked away she loudly whispered, "Plastic surgeon."

Um.

"For what?" I asked.

Olivia tapped her nose. Then she whispered, "He's a genius. Call him."

Shocked, my jaw dropped as if I'd been slapped. *Seriously? Did I look that bad?* My body tingled with embarrassment. I walked home after class, dejected. Upstairs, I washed my face and slathered it with arnica cream and googled Dr. Kaminow. I was in the midst of celebrity before and after pictures (actually, Olivia was right. Dr. Kaminow *was* the best) when the phone rang and Matt called upstairs that it was for me.

Out in the hall I picked up the extension and heard Mona's voice, a little more agitated than usual.

"Darling. So exciting. Rosner is being quite aggressive. Apparently, he likes to wrap things up on his own timetable. Anyhoo, are you free . . . tomorrow? I will pay you double for the short notice, of course. But if you could possibly fit us in?" I could hear the hope in Mona's voice, but I was feeling anything but pretty today.

"Oh . . ." I stalled. "Um . . ."

"If you *are* free, that is?" Mona asked brightly.

Oh, I was free all right. I sighed. Mona is my bread and butter. All my clothing money and social life money comes from the work I do with her. Plus, she's our steadiest cupcake customer, with a weekly order. How could I not support her in her time of need?

"Sure. What time do you need me there? And you don't have to pay me double, Mona," I added, silently grateful that Alexis could not hear me right now.

"Divine!" Mona exploded on the other end. "Just divine! I love you, you darling girl. Putting you in my will! Be here at five, please, tomorrow! Ta-ta!" she trilled, and she hung up.

I stood in the hall, staring at the phone in my hand. "Oh boy," I said out loud.

Matt was coming up the stairs behind me. "Bad news?" he asked, pausing.

I nodded. "Mona needs me for a big job tomorrow."

"How's that bad news?" he asked, confused.

I tapped my nose the same way Olivia had earlier.

"Oh. Seriously? Get over it. No one will even

notice," he said, shaking his head in disgust and continuing on to his room.

"Matthew, we are talking about people who work with beauty for a living. They'll notice all right. It's their job to make sure every little physical detail is perfect!"

"Then maybe you need to start hanging around less snobby people," he said. And he closed the door to his room behind him.

"Ugh!" I yelled in frustration. I wanted to shout, "I'm a model! They're all snobby people!" But it sounded too awful to say that out loud.

It was time for a tea bag compress and all the parsley I could handle. If only I had time for a quick visit with Dr. Kaminow!

CHAPTER 5

Gobble, Gobble

$\mathcal{I}$ was so distracted at school, I could barely concentrate on what my friends were talking about at lunch, never mind classes. Thank goodness I didn't have any tests or quizzes that day.

"Emma! Your face is looking so much better!" Katie said kindly as we all met up at our lunch table.

"Thanks," I said. "I see it too, but I think if you haven't been with me since the beginning, it still looks pretty awful."

Katie nodded sympathetically. "I guess," she agreed.

"Katie! Emma's got a big modeling job today! We all agree she looks just fine, right?" Mia said emphatically, glaring at Katie.

Katie looked mortified. "Oh! Right. Totally,

Em. And when you put on some of that concealer and stuff from Mrs. Valdes, I'm sure it will all be invisible."

"I'm wearing it now," I said, smiling.

"Oh! Well. Maybe a reapplication?" Katie said hopefully. And we all had to laugh. It felt good, and I thought about how lucky I am to have such supportive friends.

"Okay, business!" said Alexis.

"What else?" I teased.

"I spoke with Kathy Dwyer, and they'd love a cupcake donation for the party—cute and fun cupcakes, and nut free, of course."

"Great. When will we make them?" I asked.

"I've already thought of that," said Alexis. "When we do the Mona baking and the holiday boutique baking on Friday, we'll do extra frosting for another batch of Hanukkah cupcakes, and we'll make the frosting for whatever our second Christmassy-themed cupcakes are. Then we'll just have to bake the cakes Sunday morning and then frost and deliver! Voilà!"

"We can do it at my house," offered Katie. "All of it. It's fine."

We heaved a collective sigh of relief. Katie's house was the only one where we could really take over, especially more than once a week. My house was just too busy, with too many people, and Alexis's mom couldn't stand too much mess for too long, and Mia's house was busy too.

"So what should we do for the Christmas cupcakes?" I asked.

"Hmm," said Mia.

We were all quiet, thinking while we ate our lunch for a moment. Of course just then, Olivia walked by to hand in her empty tray. She inclined her head sympathetically at us and said, "Disfigurement is so sad. Stay strong, Emma." Then she shook her head with big, sad eyes and kept walking.

When she was about three paces away, we all burst out laughing.

"Disfigurement?" Alexis snorted. "Big word, Olivia! Someone's been playing with the thesaurus app!"

"I love the sympathy," agreed Mia. "So genuine."

"Oh no. Is it that bad?" I whispered. I thought I might cry suddenly.

My friends turned in unison and looked at me in shock.

"You can't be serious!" Alexis said indignantly.

I half-shrugged, not willing to trust my voice.

Katie sideways hugged me, her soup spoon

in her other hand. "Don't let the turkeys get you down. That's what my mom always says."

"Gobble, gobble!" agreed Mia.

"Quack!" I said, referring to an old inside joke about letting things roll off you like water off a duck's back.

Then we all laughed. But deep down inside, I wondered how bad it really looked. After all, my friends were used to it by now. What would Harry Rosner think?

It wasn't long before I found out.

The Special Day bridal salon was all aflutter when I arrived after school. Not that this was unusual, as they've had their fair share of important designers and clients come through. But this had a different energy—a negative one. Patricia, who is the manager and my favorite employee of all, kind of snapped at me to hurry when I got there, and though I didn't see her, I could hear Mona complaining to one of the salesgirls because the rug had some fuzz on it. It was a weird vibe.

I hurried into my usual fitting room and stopped short when I saw the dresses hanging on my rack. They were incredibly beautiful. Like beautiful fairy princess dresses for a ball (and I have seen a lot

of junior bridesmaids' dresses!). Light, delicate . . .
The word "gossamer" came to mind, which Mona
had told me meant really delicate, light fabric that
kind of floated. Exquisite, feathery lengths of tulle
draped just so, with delicate, detailed, flower rosettes
holding the folds in swags and drapes. I put on the
first dress on the rack and felt I had honestly never
looked better in my life. It was such a flattering
cut through the neckline, and just the right length.
Patricia came in when I said I was ready and gasped
when she saw me.

I put my hand to my face. "I know. The nose
is . . ."

"That is the prettiest thing I have ever seen you
wear!" she exclaimed, staring at the dress. "Simply
breathtaking!"The words rushed out as she stepped
closer to fix my hair; there seemed to be no time
for pleasantries. Then she glanced at my face in the
mirror, just really seeing me for the first time, and
did a double take.

"Yeah . . . ," I said. "About the nose . . ."

"Well, we've got no time to waste on that. Let's
just . . ." She kind of roughly started fixing my hair.

"Ow!" I said, half joking, and she softened.

"Oh my gosh, I'm so sorry, Emma. It's so crazy
in here this afternoon. It's . . ."

"Kind of a bummer!" I said lightly.

Patricia pressed her lips together and nodded. Then she said, "Yes. That's the word for it. Ever since Mr. Rosner arrived, there've been all kinds of demands. Pinker lightbulbs in the salon, tea with half and half, which he sent back because he thought we'd given him cream, turn down the music, turn up the music, and so on." She swept my hair up and looked at it critically. "Hair down, I think," she said. "Maybe a curl across the forehead to minimize. . . . Anyway, Mona's been on fire since he got here. Sniping at everyone and really just out of character. I don't know if she's trying to impress him or what . . . ," she whispered. "We're all just really cranky." She parted my hair deeply on one side, then secured it with a barrette over the other ear, so it draped dramatically over my forehead.

"Do you have any more, um, concealer?" she asked.

I started in surprise. "Oh! Sure. Let me just . . ." I bent down and dug through my bag and pulled out my tools. "I can—"

"Wait. I'll do it," said Patricia. She draped a muslin cloth over my shoulders to protect the dress, and then she used a brush to apply some more concealer over the bruising. It felt like a lot.

47

I turned to look in the mirror. It *looked* like a lot. "Should I maybe wipe some of this off?" I asked.

"No, it's dimmer in the salon than usual. Pink lightbulbs, you know?" She sighed and sat down heavily on the little stool in the dressing room. "I'm going to hide in here until you're done with that dress. You never saw me!" she joked. "Just glide on out there and do your gorgeous thing and then come on back, and I'll help you with the next look." She closed her eyes and leaned back against the wall.

"Wish me luck," I whispered. Suddenly, I was supernervous.

I tapped on the door to the private salon, and Mona trilled in a high, phony voice, "Come in!"

I entered the room and saw Mona first, dressed in a very fashionable suit. As I opened the door farther, I spied a portly, older man who was dressed way too young for his age, in intentionally beat-up designer jeans, a shiny shirt that was too tight, and really dorky tinted glasses. He had gray hair that was long and slicked back over his ears, and he was gulping loudly from one of Mona's fine teacups with a plate full of cookies in front of him and crumbs on his shirt. I guess he looked fashiony, but he also looked all wrong.

I just couldn't believe that this was the same man who had created the delicate, angelic dresses I'd found in my dressing room.

Mona was beaming a nervous smile. "Darling! Come meet Mr. Rosner! Harry, darling, this is Emma, my finest young model, showing you how we present our junior bridesmaids' looks at the salon."

Mr. Rosner looked up and nodded, more interested in the cookie he was eating.

"Hello," I said quietly.

Mona looked nervous. "Why don't you come do your twirl and step onto the box, and we'll see how it shows?" Mona suggested in a tight, bright voice.

I did as she instructed, trying my hardest to be my most graceful and swanlike and worthy of the dress. I perched on the low box that Mona has people step on for hemming, and I stood with my hands folded as charmingly as I could. I smiled.

"What happened to ya face?" Harry Rosner mumbled through a mouthful of crumbs. He had a strong accent from the city, and he barely made eye contact as he spoke.

Gosh, even in the dimness, even with him not knowing me, he saw it. Mona looked at him nervously and began to ramble in a fake-cheery voice. "There's always a liability when you're working with young models! Emma had an unfortunate meeting with a football over the weekend, but it will soon heal up and she'll be back to her usual self!"

Harry Rosner waved his hand. "She doesn't work. Get someone else!" he barked.

My hands and the soles of my feet went dead cold.

"Pardon me?" said Mona.

He swallowed and looked appraisingly at me, as if I was a side of beef he was considering for the grill. "I don't want someone defective. Get me someone good."

"But, Mr. Rosner, Emma is a beautiful young lady and our top model. Surely, anyone can see past a little bruising. . . ."

Harry Rosner stood up and approached me. It was all I could do not to run away. Mona jumped up and came to my side too. He took my chin in his hands, much as Mrs. Valdes had done on Sunday, but where she was all gentleness and care, he was rough. "She's got a pound of makeup on here! I want natural. I want fresh. I want undamaged. If you can't give me that . . . ," he warned.

I stepped down from the box and strode out of

the room. I wasn't going to stand there and let him treat me like spoiled meat, and more important, I was about to cry all over his dress.

"I take exception to your opinion, Mr. Rosner, but if you insist, I will call on someone less professional and, in my opinion, less beautiful, to come in and finish the showing with you. . . ." Mona was saying as I left the room.

"It'll have to be Saturday. I have to get going. I haven't got all day for these shenanigans . . . ," Mr. Rosner said rudely.

I stormed into the dressing room, and Patricia's head jerked up, her eyes snapping open like window shades. "Back so soon?" she said in surprise.

I struggled to take the dress off as quickly as possible without damaging it. I couldn't even speak, I was so upset. Thank goodness I'd had the dignity to storm out when I did, even though when the adrenaline wore off, I would regret not having given Mr. Rosner a piece of my mind.

"Another look? Already?" Patricia said in confusion.

And then Mona was at the door. "My darling?" she whispered. "Are you all right? I am so sorry to have put you through that. It was a terrible error in judgment on my part, all around," she said somberly.

I took a deep breath and willed myself to be composed. (Gobble, gobble! Quack!). "It's okay, Mona," I whispered.

"You will be handsomely compensated for today. And now I need to find someone else to finish this. Someone who could be here this Saturday, who's so eager for the work they'd put up with anything. Anyone . . ."

There was a brief silence. And then I said, "Call Olivia Allen."

And that was that.

You're divine!

CHAPTER 6

I'm Damaged Goods

The only thing worse than fake-sympathetic Olivia Allen is fake-sympathetic gloating Olivia Allen.

From the get-go, Wednesday was terrible. Olivia had already texted anyone she remotely knew at school to tell them that she'd been requested by *the* Harry Rosner to model, after he'd fired a "damaged" model (yours truly) who didn't meet his standards. Imagine me trying to insert myself into this—should I tell people that Mona had called Olivia "less beautiful" and that she was clearly her second choice? Should I explain how awful Harry Rosner was and that I wouldn't have wanted to work with him, anyway, not even for all the tea in China? There was no way to gracefully right the story without looking like a jerk on top of being a loser.

I hadn't had the heart to tell the Cupcakers the news the night before, so they were a little miffed to hear it through the grapevine. I cried in the bathroom twice before lunch, and once again after, when I'd actually seen Olivia face-to-face in the cafeteria. While she was in front of a not-insignificant number of people, Olivia put on a big fake-apology about "stealing" my job out from under me and how she was going to give me a good talking-to about protecting a model's "prized asset" (my face). She closed with an offer to contact Dr. Kaminow herself and put in a good word, in case I was having a hard time getting in to see him. By then, it was all I could do to nod and turn around without crying, though they were tears of anger and frustration as much as mortification.

When I got home from school, there was an envelope with twice my going rate for a full day's work, from Mona, hand delivered. I shook my head in disbelief as I looked at the amount on the check, and read her note, which said, simply: *You're divine!* —*M.*

I'd never be able to cash it, and I called her to thank her and tell her.

Mona got right on the line. "Darling, the man is a beast! I told him so in the end. I cannot understand how it is possible for him to create such beautiful work when he is filled with such ugliness. Your little friend will suffice for this weekend, but I will wait for you to heal before I schedule anything with him again...."

"Thanks, Mona, but I can't work with that horrible man," I said.

"Of course, darling. Well, I'll make it up to you, then...."

"Thanks. About the check, Mona..."

"Darling, you earned it! Combat pay! I won't take no for an answer!"

"Thanks, but I can't possibly accept this much money. I really didn't earn it."

"You certainly did. Now cash it and move on. Think of it as Harry Rosner's money. Business is business. Now go get better! Kiss, kiss!"

"Bye," I said. Mona sounded more like her usual happy self today. That Harry Rosner had brought out the worst in everyone yesterday.

Maybe I should put the money in my plastic surgery fund.

Meanwhile, it was time for some tea bags.

Thursday, Katie brought in a treat. She'd been tinkering at home, she said, playing around with some flavors and things she had on hand, and she'd come up with a couple of cupcake recipes and ideas that she'd brought in for us to try.

Now, nothing cheers me up like a good cupcake (that's how this whole thing got started, anyway), and I was happy to be a guinea pig today, especially since there was no sign of Olivia around to comment on letting my figure go too.

"Okay, this first one is called a Snowball Express," said Katie, handing them around.

It was a dense white cake with a Hershey's kiss baked into the center of it and heaps of fluffy white marshmallow frosting on top. It was so good; it was insane, as my brother Matt would say.

"Next up, Cinnamon Swirl: yellow cake studded with Red Hots baked throughout, and a pink cinnamon-spiced frosting." Katie doled them out and smiled as we tried those, too.

"Delicious!" I exclaimed. Mia and Alexis agreed.

Finally, Katie had made a red velvet cake with green cream cheese frosting on top. "Okay, this is not a new recipe but a revamp, with a sweet, seasonal design," said Katie. "Tell me which one you like best."

"It's impossible to pick!" I complained loudly. The cupcakes had made me slightly wild what with all that sugar.

Mia said, "I think the red and green ones are the prettiest."

Alexis asked sensibly, "Which one has the least expensive ingredients?"

Katie smiled again. "I'm glad you like them. Just remember, looks aren't everything. We can make any of them look pretty. Which do you think kids at the hospital will like the best?"

"The Snowball Express!" we all said in unison, and then we laughed.

"Okay, then Snowball Express it is! And they're the most expensive, Alexis!" Katie said.

"Ack!" said Alexis, grinning.

"We'll make these all for the kids instead of two types," said Katie. "So tomorrow: It's a date! My house, right after school."

I had a sudden idea. "I'll buy the supplies tonight, if you tell me what we need. It's on me."

"No, you don't need to do that!" the others began to protest, but I shushed them.

"I want to. Some unexpected money came my way, but I'm not happy about it." I grinned. "Let me put it to good use."

❀

Friday was dark and freezing cold again. My mom said that it would probably be snowing by the time I got out of school, so she insisted I wear my boots and warmest coat, and pack mittens and a hat. I felt like such a dork. But when I got to school, I was relieved to see that the other Cupcakers had dressed the same.

Luckily, my mom had agreed to drop the cupcake supplies off immediately at Katie's the night before, on our way home from the grocery store. I would not have been able to lug them to school and then on to Katie's, that was for sure.

At school, everyone was buzzing about the snow, which had not yet started.

"I heard there's going to be a blizzard," said George.

"Two feet, I heard," said Kristen Durkin.

Jeanie Parker reported in English that it had started falling, and we all ran to the window to look, even the teacher. It was coming down fast, and patches of the ground already looked whitish. At noon, the principal came on the PA system.

"Attention! Attention, students and teachers! Due to the worsening and extreme weather conditions, by order of the superintendent, school will be dismissed immediately. Please proceed in an orderly fashion. . . ."

But he was drowned out by cheers and screams and kids throwing books in the air, even! The teachers looked relieved; some of them had to drive from pretty far away, and with it being a Friday, traffic would be bad, anyway. I ran to my locker, so excited, and got my things together. We'd have less homework, too, since I was missing four classes and those teachers were big assigners. Suddenly, life was looking really good.

I was pretty sure we'd be heading straight to Katie's, so I bundled up to go search for the other Cupcakers, but when I slammed my locker door, who was standing right behind it but Olivia Allen.

Ugh!

"Hey, Em," she said, all saccharine sweet. "Just seeing what you're up to this weekend."

I pulled my hat lower on my forehead and lifted my scarf higher up my face, so that only about an inch of me was showing (granted, it was the bad inch). Olivia winced dramatically as she looked at my face.

"Oooh, Emma, it's got to just hurt so much!" she said.

"Not anymore. Don't know what I'm up to," I

mumbled through my outerwear, and I started to pass by her.

"Okay, because I'll be at the salon tomorrow and just wondered if you need anything from there? Should I put in a good word for you? Like, for when you're all better . . . after the operation?"

I wheeled around. That was it!

"Listen, Olivia! There will not be any operation. And furthermore, the only reason you got that job was because I told Mona to call you. I am still her number-one girl and she told me so, word for word, when I called her this week to thank her for paying me *double* for the work I did with Harry Rosner. Get it? So don't even mention my name to Mona or I'll . . . I'll . . . send *you* to Dr. Kaminow!" I shouted. And then I stormed off, leaving Olivia staring after me with her jaw open in exaggerated shock, shaking her head and trying to catch the eye of any passersby who might sympathize with her. In my last glance back, there were no takers.

My heart was racing, and my breath was coming so fast, I had to get out of there. I stomped down the stairs, bashed open the doors, and ran outside. A row of school buses was idling and all was pandemonium as some kids raced to make their buses while others scraped the rapidly accumulating snow into any kind of missile they could form and then launched them at one another. I wished I could throw one right in Olivia Allen's face!

I ducked under the overhang to get out of the snow, and then I pulled out my phone and sent a group text to the Cupcakers that I would meet them at Katie's. Tucking my phone snugly back into my pocket, I began trudging to Katie's on my own. I had to keep moving, because if I saw Olivia again, who knew what I might say.

It wasn't long before my adrenaline began to fade and I began to feel really cold, and then regret crept in. Had I really just threatened to basically break Olivia Allen's face? Wow. I'd been living with boys for too long. *They* were the ones who settled things with fists, not girls! Still, I had to smile, thinking of how proud they would have been if they had seen me standing up for myself. I can only be patient for so long before I totally lose it. It's not a great quality.

Lost in thought, I kicked the snow along the sidewalk as I walked, and I didn't hear the feet coming up behind me until the last minute.

"Hey, snow girl!"

The Cupcakers had sneaked up behind me and

were now jumping on me and grabbing me and joking around.

"Why'd you ditch us?" asked Alexis.

I explained what had happened with Olivia and told them how ashamed I was of my behavior.

"Ashamed? Are you kidding? She had that coming! I was wondering how much longer you were going to let it go on!" said Mia.

"Yeah, I was thinking of stepping in myself!" said Katie, flexing her arm muscle inside her parka.

"You don't think I overdid it?" I asked nervously. I couldn't stop feeling like such a jerk.

"No way. Not at all," said Alexis. "Olivia is one of those people who you have to literally bash over the head to make anything clear. She's totally alone in her own world."

"But people listen to her. She tells everyone everything!" I protested.

"Yeah, but no one *really* listens," said Mia, shaking her head. "People think Olivia is a pest. They just put up with her."

"Really?" I pressed.

"Really!" the others answered in unison.

"Come on, take a deep breath. You'll feel better," said Alexis.

"Yeah, you did the right thing," agreed Mia.

"Now, let's go get some tea bags on what's left of those bruises!" ordered Katie, giving me a sideways squeeze. "And a snack!"

"Count me in!" I cried.

CHAPTER 7

Snowy Sleepover!

There is nothing as cozy as a blizzard! Especially when it turns into a sleepover!

When it became clear that the snow was just going to pile up, Katie got permission from her mom to have us sleep over, and we all called our homes to have our parents drop off supplies when they got back from work. One by one the bags arrived, and we settled in for the long haul.

We spent the start of the afternoon by eating grilled cheese and tomato soup, and then we began baking. We owed Mona her regular order of white-on-white mini cupcakes for tomorrow, plus the two kinds for the holiday boutique and the prebaking of the Snowball Express cupcakes for Sunday. We worked like a well-oiled machine and somehow got into one of our silly cupcake games as we worked. In this one, which we call Make It Their Own, someone calls out a person's name and we all have to come up with a cupcake that sounds like them.

For example, Katie called "Mrs. Wexler!," who is our school nurse. She is supercalm, supersoothing, but a little dull.

I replied, "I'll take this! Okay, definitely thinking vanilla. Definitely something with graham crackers. Kind of dry. Mild. How about white cupcakes with vanilla pudding in the center, and vanilla frosting, with graham cracker crumble on top?"

Everyone laughed, but Katie said, "Guess what? It was a trick question! Mr. Green told me at dinner the other night that Mrs. Wexler plays in a rock band on the weekends! I keep forgetting to tell you guys!"

"No way!" we yelled.

We had a huge laugh imagining Mrs. Wexler rocking out, and I changed my vanilla pudding center to spicy cinnamon syrup (because she has a wild private life under that plain exterior), which made us all laugh even harder.

I went next. "Okay, here's mine. Olivia Allen!"

"Ooooh!" said Mia. "How about something

hideous like pineapple upside-down cake with chunky pumpkin frosting, and some kind of little seed sprinkled on it that gets stuck in your teeth and annoys you for the rest of the day?"

"That's awesome," I said. "Totally annoying—like Olivia!"

"What about Matt Taylor?" asked Alexis, with a smile.

"Oh no! I can't hear this one!" I said, covering my ears with my hands like earmuffs.

"No, it will be good," said Katie. "Don't worry."

"Well, it should really be bacon cupcakes, since those are his favorites, like they're Emma's," said Mia.

"Maybe blueberries in a corn muffin cupcake, like his blue eyes and blond hair . . . ," said Alexis dreamily.

"Oh gag!" I said. I rolled my eyes.

"How about lemon cupcakes with a mocha frosting?" offered Katie. "You know, blond but strong." She shrugged.

"Hmm. It's okay, but not beautiful enough," said Alexis.

"How about a Snowball Express?" I shouted. "Because I think it's a good time for a snowball fight!"

We looked around the kitchen and saw that we were in very good shape. There were no cupcakes in the oven; everything we had already made was cooling on racks on every surface. The frosting was ready to go, and we had the whole late evening ahead of us to finish.

"Let's do it!" yelled Mia, who was already pulling on her boots.

Soon we were all outside, screaming and laughing, making snow forts to protect us and piling up arsenals of snowballs. Mia and I took on Katie and Alexis, and we were pretty evenly matched. We were outside for almost an hour, and we were sopping wet by the end of it: freezing and exhausted.

Mrs. Brown pulled up with a carload of shopping bags and war stories from the crazed aisles of the grocery store where people were panicking to buy supplies.

"I got the last box of popcorn on the shelves!" she said, pretending to stagger with exhaustion against the side of her car.

"Yay, Mrs. Brown!" I yelled.

We helped her bring the things inside, and then we all dispersed to take hot showers and change into dry pj's. Mrs. Brown was going to make chili with corn bread, and then we'd be watching a movie after dinner.

Back in the kitchen all toasty and cozy, we finished frosting and decorating the holiday boutique cupcakes and the minis for Mona and then boxed them all up in our cupcake carriers (one of the hardest things about our club is remembering which house we left the carriers at. Luckily, this time Alexis had them, and her mom was able to drop them off with Alexis's bag). We helped Mrs. Brown with the chili prep, and Mia made the corn bread and popped it in the oven, then we sat around while the chili bubbled on the stove and the corn bread baked, and we talked with Mrs. Brown.

"Emma, honey, your eyes are looking really good!" she said.

"Thanks," I agreed. "The stuff you sent helped so much."

"Thank you for your sweet note," she said.

"I couldn't believe how well the arnica worked. By the next day the bruising was visibly better."

"All those remedies are pretty amazing. You have to figure there must be a natural cure on Earth for every natural cause, you know? I mean, I'm not sure about diseases that might be man-made or man-influenced, but certainly allergies and aches and pains and irritations. I think modern medicine hasn't scratched the surface of what's available on this planet."

"Yeah. My mom thinks so too," I agreed.

Mrs. Brown looked at me closely. "I'd say you're probably only one good application of arnica away from total healing."

I agreed. "And Mrs. Valdes's concealer is really doing the trick now that the bruising is so mild."

"I'm happy it all worked out," Mrs. Brown said with a warm smile.

"I'm lucky to have such good friends with such nice moms to help me!" I agreed.

"Yeah, imagine if Olivia Allen was your friend!" said Alexis. "She'd probably punch you in the nose again the second you started looking better!"

"To steal all your work!" added Katie.

"Now, girls! Be nice!" warned Mrs. Brown.

"Oh, but, Mom, you have to understand ...," said Katie, and she explained all about Harry Rosner and Olivia and Dr. Kaminow.

Mrs. Brown listened thoughtfully as she checked the chili and corn bread. Then she said, "You know, it sounds like Olivia doesn't have much to go on in life. Who are her good friends?"

We all looked at one another. We couldn't name

one. I shrugged. "I think she doesn't really have any. Well, maybe Callie and those girls." Then I stopped. Callie Wilson and Katie used to be best friends before middle school, but Callie started hanging out with girls who called themselves the Popular Girls and that was pretty much the end of that friendship. But now Katie seemed okay with it.

"But, Mom, it's her own fault!" protested Katie. "You have to see her in action."

Mrs. Brown shrugged. "Some people are insensitive or awkward or nervous, and they blurt out dumb things or wrong things, but I don't think Olivia sounds like a truly mean person. Lost, maybe, or vain, misguided, but certainly trying to be helpful and included. Trying to be a part of your world. I could be wrong," she said, shrugging again. "Just remember, especially at this time of year, to be sympathetic to people and to do your best to be kind."

We were all quiet for a moment as we took in this advice. I felt bad, a little, for what I'd said at school.

"Well, as long as Olivia would do her best too, maybe she'd have some friends . . . ," said Katie, trailing off.

"You girls are so lucky to have one another," said Mrs. Brown. "You don't even realize it!"

"Oh, we realize it all right!" said Alexis.

"All right, then, good! So run along, and I'll call you when this is ready in a bit. Go do something fun," Mrs. Brown said with a twinkle in her eyes. "Enough serious stuff for now! Don't you know this is a blizzard sleepover?"

"Woo-hoo!" we all cheered, and we scampered up the stairs to Katie's room.

But I couldn't help wondering as I climbed the steep staircase what Olivia was doing right now to celebrate the blizzard. If I had to guess, she was probably home alone. Part of me thought, *Well, you reap what you sow.* But another, better, part of me thought, *What if the next time I see her, maybe, just maybe, I'll assume she's trying to be nice . . . and I'll just be nice back.*

The rest of the night passed in a very cozy fashion. We ate our delicious dinner around the dining room table; Mrs. Brown had lit a fire in the fireplace in there, and it was so warm and snug. After dinner, we roasted marshmallows over the open fire to make s'mores, and then we settled in to watch a romantic comedy we'd been meaning to see for a while.

During a boring part of the movie, I looked

around at my besties and tried to think of what I could buy them for Christmas. I had some money left over from the Rosner nonjob, so I could go to the mall and pick up some stuff; maybe fancy hand creams or barrettes, maybe even a small iTunes gift card for each girl. But I couldn't get excited about any of those ideas. It all seemed impersonal and useless—something they'd never remember, something that wouldn't mean anything to them, something that would be used up or lost or thrown away. How would it honor my friends to give them plastic junk?

If I could make them something, that would be cool. But what? I'm not a knitter. I sewed a skirt in school, but I doubted I could really make anything more complicated than that. I could bake them something, but all I really know are cupcakes, and that seems a little silly. Something with beads? There was a cool new bead store at the mall that I'd been meaning to check out. But beads can be a lot of work, and I don't have a whole lot of time left.

As I cast my thoughts around, I decided that maybe I'd get inspired at the holiday boutique tomorrow. Maybe there'd be something I could buy them there. Something rare and special—just like them!

CHAPTER 8

Homemade Goodies

We were up early Saturday morning because the light was coming in so bright around Katie's shades. She got up first and snapped open the first shade to peek outside, and the light came flooding in, reflected off the snow on the ground.

"You guys, come look!" cried Katie.

One by one we groaned and got up and peered out the frosted windowpane. It was a winter wonderland outside: The tree branches were thickly lined with ribbons of snow, and it was massed in big drifts against the fence and shrubs in the yard. Down the street, a parked car was being farther snowed in on the street by a pickup pushing a huge plow at the front. The plow scraped along the pavement, and I realized that was the sound I'd been hearing, semiconscious, all night.

"Wow! I wonder if the holiday boutique is still on," said Alexis. "I'd better get in touch with the organizer."

"It's so beautiful," I said. "We should make snowmen."

"Yes!" agreed Katie.

"I don't have any more dry clothes, I think," said Mia.

"Yeah." Alexis looked at her watch. "Anyway, it's eight o'clock. We've got to get Mona's minis to her by nine and over to the boutique—if it's on—by ten."

"Slave driver!" teased Katie.

"All work and no play . . . ," I singsonged.

"All play and no work makes us all broke at holiday time!" Alexis singsonged back at me, and I had to laugh.

We cleaned up Katie's room and sorted our stuff back into our bags, and then we went downstairs.

Mrs. Brown was at the table reading the news on her laptop. "I can't believe you're all up so bright and early!" she said. "I was shocked when I heard you all moving around up there. Why not sleep late?"

We explained everything we had to do and

about halfway through our itinerary, Mrs. Brown laughed and took one last swig of her tea, standing up and shutting her computer all in one fell swoop. "I think I'd better go get dressed so I can take you. Good thing I have four-wheel-drive!"

"Thanks, Mom!" said Katie. Then, as her mom left the room, Katie whispered, "Phew! I'd forgotten to ask if she could take us!"

"Your mom would never leave us hanging. She's the best," I said.

"All our moms are the best!" Mia said emphatically.

"None of them would ever leave us hanging!" agreed Alexis.

"It's true. To our moms!" I said, toasting them with orange juice.

Everyone joined in. "To the best moms in the world!" agreed Katie.

On the drive to Mona's, I realized I could not take the cupcakes in today, of course, because Harry Rosner was scheduled to be there for the modeling session with Olivia! The other Cupcakers understood but felt that I shouldn't let Olivia push me out of my rightful place as the number-one junior bridesmaid model at The Special Day.

Mrs. Brown said I was welcome to wait in the car with her, and even though I felt like a bit of a chicken, I did just that. The girls were gone a little bit longer than I would have thought, and when they came back, they were scrambling over one another with wild news for me. Everyone was talking at once.

"Okay, wait! What happened?" I said.

"Katie, you tell," said Mia.

"Okay. Listen to this!" she said as Mrs. Brown began to drive out of the mall's parking lot. "We go in. Mona's there, but she's all stressed and in a bad mood. . . ."

"That's Harry Rosner for you!" I said, shaking my head.

"Right!" said Katie. "So we also saw Olivia. She was in a really beautiful dress, and she actually looked . . . well, I hate to admit it, but she did look really pretty. Anyway, she followed into that private salon room, and a minute later, the Rosner guy comes storming out, with Mona right behind him. So he starts yelling, 'Why can't you get me a really beautiful girl? Why is it so hard? Someone like . . .' and then, Emma, you'll never believe what he did!"

Katie paused for dramatic effect. All the girls' eyes were shining brightly.

"What?" I urged. "What?"

"He pointed to that big gorgeous blown-up photo of you on the wall and said, 'Someone like her!'"

Katie and the girls all burst out laughing.

"Oh no!" I said, covering my face with my hands. "I can't believe it!"

Katie nodded. "Totally. So Mona, well . . . Mona went a little nuts, actually. She basically kicked him out of the store, right, you guys?"

Alexis cut in. "Yes, she said, 'Mr. Rosner, it is a shame your dresses are so beautiful and you are such an ugly person. I cannot work with you. Please leave at once and instruct my staff how you would like the dresses returned to you. Good day!'"

"And then she turned and walked away, back into the salon!" added Mia.

They stared at me, gloating.

I couldn't believe it. "Wow! I wish I'd been there."

"It was really good. Mona was great. And all the staff—Patricia, and the salesgirls—they just stood there with their jaws open."

"And what did you guys do? Did you ask for our money?"

"No! We left!" Alexis shrieked with laughter.

77

"No way!" I had to laugh too. "You just sneaked out the door? Alexis? You walked away from money?"

Alexis howled. "Desperate times call for desperate measures!" she said.

"But wait"—I suddenly realized—"what about Olivia?"

The girls all fell silent.

"Um. We never saw her again," Katie said in a small voice.

"We kind of forgot that part," agreed Mia.

"She must've been mortified. I mean, how could she not have known that he was rejecting her?" I asked, feeling an unusual burst of sympathy for Olivia.

"Gosh, you're right," agreed Alexis, all sobered up. "That's pretty harsh."

"No kidding!" I said. "It happened to me, and I felt awful. I wish I had stuck up for myself. I hope Olivia did."

"Hey! Emma! I just realized!" cried Katie, peering intently at me from the front seat. "Your nose! Your eyes! You're all back to normal!"

"Really?" I asked.

I'd been in such a hurry to get ready, I'd forgotten to check before we left the house. I leaned up to look in the visor's mirror Katie had flipped down for me.

"She's right. It's really gone," agreed Mia.

"I can't tell from here," I said, sitting back. "But I hope you're right."

"Em, you look good all the time, anyway," Katie said sweetly.

The others agreed. "Thanks. Maybe you all could give Harry Rosner some pointers," I said with a grin.

"Totally," agreed Alexis.

I was pretty distracted for the rest of the ride over to the holiday boutique. I couldn't help feeling bad for Olivia since I knew just what she'd gone through. A tiny part of me was flattered about what Mr. Rosner said, even though it revealed that he was clearly nuts, but I was embarrassed for Olivia and sympathetic to how Mona must've felt too. They were really better off without him, though, no matter how beautiful his clothes were. It was weird that such a nasty man could make something so pretty, I thought again. Mrs. Brown dropped us outside the Y where the boutique was being held and promised to come back and get us at midday. The organizer had told Alexis we could man our own table until noon, and then they'd hand it off to some other kids who needed community service hours and were eager for the work. That sounded just perfect to us, since it would give us time to do a little shopping and get home in time for lunch.

Despite the storm, the place was a hive of activity and good cheer. People who'd been stranded en route to the fair were straggling in with tales of the kindnesses of strangers, and the vendors were looking to help one another, sharing easels and change and cooperating in all sorts of ways to make things work out.

The hall had been decorated beautifully in a green and white theme—with swags of seasonal greenery and potted evergreens and tiny electric candles everywhere. It was very festive and it smelled great from all the plants and baked goods and things people were selling, from spiced nuts, artisanal cheeses, hand-dipped chocolates, and crumbly biscuits to handmade candles and potpourri, and organic soaps and scented creams. A volunteer directed us to our table, number forty-seven, where a thick white felt tablecloth had been laid. Mia cleverly plucked a few stray evergreen branches and laid them artistically around the table, and then

Katie set out the cupcakes on white platters. I unwrapped a package of red and green napkins I'd bought at the grocery store (we like to provide thematic or color-coordinated party goods sometimes as part of our cupcake delivery), and Alexis set up our cash box.

There were only two chairs for us, and it was a little tight behind the table as we were hemmed in from behind by a table with handmade woolly sheep decorations and on either side by a wooden puzzle maker and a needlepoint lady, so we would have to take turns selling. That left two of us at a time free to roam the aisles and see what was there.

I volunteered to sell first, as did Alexis, and Katie and Mia set off excitedly. Once the doors opened to the public at ten, business was surprisingly steady.

"Gosh, we could have sold double what we brought," Alexis muttered after only our fifth customer.

"Well, maybe it's the morning rush and things will die down later?" I said to comfort her. Alexis took missed business opportunities pretty hard, and they could set her off into a funk if she thought we had been sloppy or hadn't tried hard enough. (Her family motto is: Beckers try harder.)

She shook her head sadly. "No. It will only get busier. Oh well. Live and learn."

Business picked up then, and we didn't have a chance to really talk for a while. Mia and Katie circled past to update us on what they'd found, but we didn't have long to chat.

"People are freaking out over the cherry pistachio!" I said to Katie.

"Yay!" She glowed happily.

"There's so much great stuff to buy out there!" enthused Mia. "If only it wasn't so expensive!"

An hour in, we traded places, and I was super-excited to go see what was around. I knew the holiday boutique would be far superior to the mall when it came to buying unique gifts for my friends, and I had money in my pocket. And sure enough, everywhere we looked, there were exquisite handmade things, and Alexis and I oohed and aahed over all of them. But in the end, I wasn't able to find anything for my friends that wasn't outrageously expensive. It made sense, I guess, because people had put a lot of time and effort into these things, and they really were works of art. But two hundred and fifty dollars for a fur bunny neck warmer? Eighty dollars for hand-knit cashmere socks? It was too depressing. I couldn't believe grown-ups were buying the stuff!

I did end up buying a jar of local honey for my mom for her tea, and a really pretty raw silk coin purse with a mother-of-pearl button closure for Mona, but that was it. I was a little disheartened when I decided to return to the others, but I was looking forward to hearing that we'd made some money selling the cupcakes. I rounded the aisle to head back to table number forty-seven, and who should I spy standing right there buying a cupcake from Mia but Olivia Allen!

CHAPTER 9

Friends

"Uh, hi!" I said, approaching the table warily. I wasn't sure if Olivia would be mean or civil after what I'd said to her yesterday at school.

"Hey, Emma!" said Katie all fake-cheery, like *Please don't make a scene here!*

Olivia turned. "Wow. Your face," she said.

My hands flew instinctively to the bridge of my nose. "What?" I asked anxiously. Was it bleeding again?

"It's all better," she said, blinking.

I dropped my hand. "Oh. Yeah. Pretty much."

"That's good," she said, shrugging.

I was dying to ask her about this morning, but I didn't know if I should let on what I knew. It seemed like no one knew what to say for a second.

And then, "How was it out there?" Mia asked me, to change the subject.

"Expensive," I said dejectedly.

"Yeah," agreed Olivia. Hmm. I remembered what Katie's mom had said. Maybe she *was* trying to be nice.

"Hey, Olivia," I ventured. "I'm sorry about what I said yesterday at school." I gulped.

Olivia shrugged again. "That's okay. I understand that when someone feels ugly on the outside, it can make them a little ugly on the inside, too."

O-kaaaay. I took a deep, deep breath and thought about Mrs. Brown's advice to assume Olivia was just being awkward. So I said, "Yeah. Anyway. Sorry." It took a lot of self-control, I'll tell you.

Just then Olivia's mom came over. "Olivia," Mrs. Allen said sharply. "You shouldn't be eating cupcakes! You'll spoil your skin *and* your figure, and then you'll *really* never get hired again! What*ever* can you be thinking?" And she plucked the half-eaten cupcake out of Olivia's hand and wrapped it in one of our napkins.

Olivia stood there mutely while the rest our jaws dropped. Mrs. Allen looked around at us. "Are these the friends you were saying you wanted to invite to our holiday party?" she asked Olivia loudly.

Olivia looked embarrassed and angry, all at once.

"Mom, let's just go . . . ," she said.

The Cupcakers all exchanged mortified looks. Friends? Us?

"Wait a minute now. Not so fast! Why don't we give them the details?" continued Mrs. Allen.

Olivia was tugging on her mom's arm to get her to leave, and her face was turning red.

Quickly, I blurted, "So, Olivia, we'll pick you up tomorrow around two o'clock for the event at the children's unit of the hospital, okay?"

She looked at me blankly, but it shut her mother up.

Alexis quickly caught my drift and said, "You know. You're coming with us to volunteer at the holiday party tomorrow for the kids at the hospital, remember?"

Olivia looked at us suspiciously, and her mother said, "What's all this?"

"Wait, did I not send out that e-mail?" I said, smacking myself in the forehead.

"No, I never got it," said Mia, playing along.

"Me neither," said Katie, looking totally confused. "There was an e-mail?"

"Okay, well, my mom is driving the minivan, so we have room. I'll pick you all up around two tomorrow, more or less, and we'll go for about an hour and hand out the cupcakes to the sick kids. Got it?"

The Cupcakers all nodded emphatically.

"Okaaay . . . thanks?" said Olivia.

"No prob!" I said cheerily. "And don't forget to send us the e-mail about your holiday party. We'd love to come!" I added.

Olivia smiled in surprise. "Really? I mean, great! Okay. It's next weekend. I'll send you the info soon, I promise. See you tomorrow!" She practically skipped away down the aisle.

As soon as she rounded the bend, I turned to look at my friends.

"That was really nice of you, Em," Mia said quietly.

"Yeah, quick thinking!" said Alexis.

"I . . . am not really sure what just happened there, but obviously you just did something really kind, Emma," added Katie.

"Thanks. Sorry. I just felt so bad for her. And her mom really is torture. Nothing like our moms, you know?"

The other Cupcakers nodded.

"She's not as lucky," agreed Katie.

"Thanks for playing along, for getting it so

quickly. You guys are the best!" I said.

"No, you are!" said Mia, grabbing me in a hug. "And your face really is back to normal, by the way."

"Thanks. But I forgot when I was fibbing that we have to go to Katie's first to finish making the cupcakes! So I guess we'll just pick up Olivia after that."

"Perfect," we all agreed.

After the holiday boutique, Mrs. Brown brought us all to Katie's to pick up our stuff, and we each headed home. I was pretty tired and looking forward to chilling at home and doing some homework, just to get it out of the way.

My mom hugged me when I walked in and said, "I missed you, angel!" and that made me hug her back extra hard.

"There's a message for you on the answering machine," she said. "From Mona."

"Interesting," I said, and went to play it.

"*Hello*, darling. It's Mona for Emma. Darling, just to tell you I've finished with that loathsome man and will never work with him again. I cannot *wait* for you to come back to me for a show next week. Please ring to let me know if you're free next Saturday. We've got a *lovely* designer's things to show, and she's as sweet as Mother Teresa. No more mean people! My apologies again for that horrible episode and kiss, kiss to you all, darlings! Ciao!"

I smiled. I was back in business!

"What was that all about?" asked my mom.

I reminded her about the Harry Rosner thing and told her what had happened this morning, then I filled her in on the rest of my day and, while I was at it, all the Olivia Allen stuff.

"Sweetheart! Why didn't you tell me any of this? I feel so awful that you've been going through this all alone!"

"I haven't been all alone, Mom! I have my friends!"

My mom smiled. "Yes, it's true. I guess you do." She rubbed my back and gave me a squeeze, and I stood up to go get some work done.

Just after lunch on Sunday, we were back in Katie's kitchen, finishing the Snowball Express cupcakes.

"Your mom is so nice to let us take over your house for basically the whole weekend," I said.

Katie shrugged. "It's awfully quiet without you guys here." She thickly spread white frosting onto a cupcake and set it in the carrier. I was busy opening packages of napkins and stowing them in a small shopping bag, so they'd be ready to go when we got there. They were cute, with pictures of white fluffy snowmen against a dark-blue night sky. We thought the kids would like them. They were cheerful. Mia had brought some pine branches to lay around the cupcakes, and Alexis had three big white plastic platters we used regularly for parties.

Alexis finished wiping out the final carrier and set it down, and we all loaded the remaining cupcakes into it.

"Guys, I just have to tell you all, I'm still stumped on the holiday gifts for you," I said.

"Please! Don't get us anything!" said Mia.

"I want to. I just thought I'd luck out yesterday, and then it was an epic fail."

"It's the last thing you should be worrying about at this time of the year," agreed Alexis.

"What should we be worrying about? Year-end tax write-offs?" teased Mia.

"Well, one thing we do have to worry about is logistics when we get to the party," said Alexis. "Here's what we'll do. We can each take a carrier, and we'll find Kathy Dwyer, and she will show us where to set up. Then I think we should decide if we want to use all three platters and put out every cupcake, or just do one and keep refilling it. I think there will be tons of kids, so maybe the first option is better."

We were quiet for a moment, thinking about logistics, and then Mrs. Brown called from the other room "Emma! Your mom's here!" and it was time for us to go.

We bustled into our jackets and out to the car, crunching over the now-icy snow in the driveway, and we secured the cupcake carriers with bungee cords in the cargo area, then we set off to pick up Olivia.

As soon as we pulled into the driveway of her pretty white house, Olivia popped out the door, calling something back over her shoulder (probably promising her mom she wouldn't eat any cupcakes, I thought), and came bounding out to the van.

"Hey, everyone!" she said, clambering in. The automated door whirred shut behind her as she found a seat. Everyone greeted her warmly, which was nice. Olivia looked like she'd taken extra care with her appearance today. Her hair was in two cute braids with red bows at the ends, and she had on a white turtleneck that was sprigged with tiny Christmas trees, and a cute fuzzy holiday sweater topped with a white down vest.

"I love your outfit!" said Mia. "So cute!"

"And the braids!" added Katie.

"Thanks," said Olivia. "I actually brought some supplies in case any of the kids want me to do their hair." She patted her hobo bag at her side.

"Oh. Wow. That was a good idea," I said.

Olivia shrugged. "Sometimes it helps to do something fun with the kids. Like an icebreaker."

"How did you think of that?" I asked.

"Oh, my cousin was really sick when we were little, so I used to go visit her at the children's hospital a lot for a while. The kids there can get really bored, but they don't always feel well enough to be entertained."

"Oh," I said. "That's . . . hard."

Olivia nodded. "Yeah. You'll find out," she added. "The only thing I can't really deal with is blood, but you don't see much of that in the children's ward."

I'm not good with blood either. I thought back to when Olivia and I had both fainted at the hospital after seeing blood (I was with Jake, who was getting tested for a tonsillectomy; she was trying out to model for a blood drive poster. It was not pretty). I hadn't really been focused on the *hospital* part of the equation before this instant. I kept thinking "kids" and "holiday" and "party," but thinking about being at the hospital and that the kids might be actually really be sick suddenly made me feel nervous. Like, how should I act around them? And should I ask about how they were feeling? And would something make me faint?

The minivan pulled into the main parking area of the hospital just as a kid was being pushed out in a wheelchair. Her eyes were closed and her head was tipped back, and she looked exhausted. In my heart, I said a little prayer that she had a broken leg or something and was just tired from all the X-rays, and then the van stopped and I jumped out to get the cupcakes, all nervous energy now.

We said bye to my mom, and Alexis led the way to the desk where Kathy Dwyer had instructed her to go, and then we were onboard the world's biggest and slowest elevator, heading to the kids' ward on the top floor.

As the doors opened, I took a deep, calming breath and followed Alexis to the left, with the rest of the Cupcakers and Olivia. Katie and Mia had stopped talking on the elevator, and I realized they were nervous too, but Olivia and Alexis kept chatting away.

Down the hall, we followed the directions to

the playroom and could suddenly hear Christmas music and cheerful voices, which relaxed me a little. I tried not to look in any of the patients' rooms as we passed, because I didn't want to seem nosy or like I was gawking or invading their privacy. So when we got to the playroom, I was relieved to look up and all around.

It was a sunny, cheerful room, with a whole wall of windows looking out over a park at the edge of town, and there was a big menorah and a decorated Christmas tree, and cute paper decorations pinned all around the walls. It kind of felt like a preschool classroom.

None of the kids were there yet, but Kathy Dwyer came over to greet us warmly and introduce us to the child-life coordinators, who help with schooling and entertainment, among other things, for kids staying at the hospital. There were also a couple of nurses and two parent volunteers. Everyone was superfriendly and bubbly, and I immediately began to relax. Kathy thought one platter was probably the better way to go, so we loaded it up and stowed the carriers under the tables. There was lots of other food—sandwiches, salads, cookies—but ours was the prettiest, if I did say so myself.

And then it was time for the kids to come! My palms were actually a little sweaty, and Katie and Mia both had big, nervous smiles plastered on their faces, which was how I must've looked too. But as the first few kids came in—two in wheelchairs with IVs and one with a shaved head, on crutches— Olivia stepped forward to greet them warmly, and we all followed her, and it suddenly wasn't as scary as it had been.

Thank goodness we brought her! I thought. *I never would have believed it.*

CHAPTER 10

Angela

By the middle of the party, everyone was saying "Thank goodness for Olivia," even Kathy Dwyer. Talk about seeing a new side of a person! Olivia was comfortable from the get-go, chatting with the kids, making them laugh, bringing them things to eat and drink.

Only around eight kids came to the party, but they'd all made an effort to be festive. Some were dressed up in fancy holiday outfits, some had wrapped tinsel around their crutches, and others had snowman stickers on their casts. They all loved the cupcakes, especially the chocolate surprise in the middle.

Kathy came over to check on us at the refreshment table at one point and said, "Don't forget to smile and wave for the camera!" She pointed at a security-type camera up on the wall.

"Um, is that so the security people can get a good look at us?" I asked. "'Cause, we're pretty good kids!"

Kathy laughed. "No! It's for the kids who can't get out of their beds. They watch the events and entertainment on their TVs."

My head snapped back up to look at the camera. "Wait, what? There are sick kids watching the party on TV right now? How many?"

"Oh, about twenty," said Kathy, turning to smile and wave at the camera.

I thought I might burst into tears right then and there.

"So . . . what do they do to celebrate?" I asked.

"Usually, we bring the party to them," said Kathy. "So for example, after Santa comes here, he'll go from room to room and hand out little gifts and chat with the kids. . . ."

"And what about the refreshments and stuff?" I asked.

"We usually just put it in the staff room after, and the nurses love it."

"Well . . . could we bring some cupcakes around, or are the kids too sick to eat them?" I asked.

"Oh, certainly!" said Kathy. "Most of the time their parents will come pick up a plate for them, but if you'd like to do that, it would be lovely. I'd say most of the kids we have right now"—she squinted up at the ceiling as she thought—"can have cup-cakes!"

"Okay, great!" I said, now wondering what I'd gotten myself into. Hospitals, sick kids, potential blood . . . not my strong suit. Time to call in the reinforcements.

"Olivia!" I called. "Hey, Olivia!"

Olivia turned from where she was laughing with a little girl who seemed pretty okay, and I waved her over. I explained what Kathy and I had been talking about and asked if she'd do it with me and she readily agreed.

"Sure! Those are the kids who really need company!" she said.

"And cupcakes!" I added.

I went to tell the others what we were doing, and they all thought it was a great idea, but all three of them were too nervous to join us. Alexis agreed she'd hold down the fort, and I grabbed a cupcake carrier full of Snowball Express cupcakes while Olivia grabbed a stack of napkins. We crossed the room to check in with Kathy, who gave us our marching orders (including a list of which room numbers to visit), and we set off.

"How many?" asked Olivia as we turned right into the hallway, following Kathy's directions.

"Twelve," I said.

"Wow. That's a lot of kids!"

"To be sick. I know," I agreed. We were silent for a minute, thinking about it, and then I looked at my list and realized we'd reached the first room.

The door was halfway closed, and there was only a dim light coming from inside.

"Knock, knock," I whispered, tapping on the door. My stomach was in knots. I was so worried about what we'd find behind the door and how we'd react to it.

Quickly, a young man was at the door. He opened it, nodding at us, and gestured for us to enter. We hesitated, since he wasn't speaking, and we pointed at the cupcakes and asked if anyone might want one. Again, he waved us in, so we entered the room.

It was dim, with only one light on in the corner, and cool, and there was a whooshing sound going regularly. As we rounded the corner from the entryway, we spied a tiny girl inside a huge, clear plastic tent.

"Pneumonia," said the man, thumping his own chest. "Alexandra, sweetheart. You have some visitors." He reached the bedside and gently unzipped a wall of the tent.

"Go on, you can get in, make yourself at home," he said, like a totally normal host, as if we weren't being invited into a tent in a hospital with a tiny child.

I hung back and let Olivia go first. "Hi, Alexandra," she said in a soft but friendly voice.

The tiny girl nodded, a mask over her face. She couldn't have been more than four years old.

"We're sorry you don't feel well," said Olivia.

I looked at Olivia, then said, "We brought you a holiday treat. We can put it on your table here if you'd like." She had a wheeled convenience table pulled up alongside her bed. It was covered with coloring books and crayons that seemed untouched. The child was so thin and pale, she probably didn't have any extra energy for anything. Alexandra nodded slightly at my offer, so I opened the carrier and busied myself with the cupcake transfer.

Meanwhile, Olivia started to chatter in a quiet but upbeat voice, engaging Alexandra with yes or no questions that she was able to answer by nodding or shaking her head. Pretty soon, the questions were funny, and Alexandra was giggling behind her mask. Olivia showed Alexandra her braids with the bows and offered to braid Alexandra's own, long brown hair, and Alexandra nodded.

I could see that this wouldn't be a superquick visit, so I set down the carrier and waited while Olivia got the okay from Alexandra's dad to go ahead. Pretty soon, Alexandra had two long braids down either side of her head, each with a big red bow at the end. Olivia withdrew a mirror from her bag and let Alexandra look at her reflection. Alexandra giggled again, looking at herself, and lifted her mask to say "I love them," turning her head this way and that so she could see the braids from all angles. "Thank you."

"You look beautiful," I said, noticing that a little pink had come into Alexandra's cheeks.

Olivia said, "Well, we don't want to tire you out, and anyway, I heard a rumor that the big guy in the red suit might be coming to see you soon. . . ."

Alexandra's eyes lit up, and she nodded.

"Okay, then. We'll be on our way. Happy holidays!" Olivia said cheerfully.

"Bye!" I said, smiling a little awkwardly.

I picked up the carrier and we came out of the tent. Alexandra's dad was grinning. "Thank you so much. She hasn't been that animated since . . . well, since she got sick." His voice caught in his throat for a minute, and he paused. "Thank you. That was wonderful," he said. (I was so relieved that he didn't cry!)

"It was fun. She's adorable," said Olivia, totally relaxed and natural.

"Yes, she is," said Alexandra's dad, glancing over his shoulder.

"Happy holidays," I said with a smile.

"And to you too, girls. To you too," he said as we left.

Outside Alexandra's room, I looked at Olivia, impressed. "You were really good with her!" I said.

Olivia shrugged. "Like I said, I've had lots of bedside practice. Just as long as there's no blood around, I'm fine."

"I agree," I said, feeling queasy just thinking about it.

We made our way through three more rooms that were pretty easy (a little boy with asthma in another tent; a field hockey player with a broken leg in traction and who was thrilled to have her hair braided; and a rather spunky three-year-old boy who'd just had an appendectomy). Everyone had cupcakes, including the parents, and I told

Olivia I'd go back to get the other, full carrier and meet her in the next room.

By this point, I'd started to take my cue from Olivia. Light chatting, no pity, don't focus on why the kids are there. Don't use the word "sick," and some other little details I'd noticed, like not sitting on the bed unless invited, and stuff.

Back at the playroom, I waved at Alexis, Mia, and Katie, who were making Christmas ornaments and dreidels with the kids at the party (hard to tell who was having more fun), and swapped out the carriers. Kathy bustled over to see how it was going, and I told her it was great and that we were about halfway done.

I walked briskly back down the hall to the room where I'd told Olivia I'd meet her, but there was no one in there—the rooms was clean and empty. I looked at the list from Kathy. Maybe she'd meant the next room?

"Olivia?" I called, out in the hall. I ducked my head slightly into the next room, where I could hear a TV playing on low. "Olivia?"

"Emma?" called Olivia. She sounded kind of weird. Like a little . . . panicky. I pushed open the door fully and walked into the room with the cupcakes, and what I saw took my breath away.

It was a girl about our age, lying in the bed asleep, her face a zigzag of stitches, some of it swaddled in bandages. Her entire face was bright red and swollen and it all looked like it had just happened. A huge gash ran across her temple, and there was one down the underside of her jaw. Her right ear was wrapped in gauze that also circled her head.

"Um . . ." I kind of staggered when I saw her.

"Hi, honey," said a woman I hadn't seen. She was curled in a chair by the window, as if she'd been asleep. "This is Angela. We weren't expecting any visitors today, but we're happy to see you." She sat up and fussed with her hair, straightening her sweater.

Olivia was standing in mute shock at the foot of the bed, staring at the girl, like she'd been turned to stone by the sight of her.

"Olivia!" I whispered sharply. She looked at me and kind of snapped out of it, but she didn't do or say anything. Now what? She'd been the leader on all of this: calm, cool, and collected, and cheerful, too. I took a deep breath. I had to do or say something. I started rambling.

"We're volunteers from the holiday party down the hall," I said. "I'm Emma and this is Olivia. We're delivering cupcakes. Would Angela like one?" I asked. "Or would you?"

The woman stood up, and I could see that she was tall and elegant, with a very beautiful, if exhausted, face.

"That's so sweet. Thank you. Maybe we could take two and save them for a little later, when she wakes up," said the woman.

"Sure," I said in a cheery but quiet voice. I couldn't tell if Angela waking up would be a good thing or a bad thing, but I was pretty sure she wouldn't be eating cupcakes anytime in the near future. Still, I was glad for a task, so I busied myself with opening the carrier, and glanced at Olivia. She was still staring at Angela.

"Olivia! Napkins, please!" I said in a kind of bossy voice.

"Oh," said Olivia, turning away from Angela and looking for a place to lay down two napkins.

"Here is fine, thanks," said the woman, gesturing to a shelf on the wall.

I set out the cupcakes and then, seeing as how we couldn't really chat with Angela and Olivia certainly couldn't braid her hair, we turned to the woman to say good-bye. But on turning, I could see that she had started to weep quietly.

Olivia and I looked at each other, and Olivia seemed terrified. I took a deep breath and said the first thing that came to my mind. "Would you like a hug? We're handing those out too."

The woman laughed a little and said, "Sure, I'd love one. I'm so sorry. I keep losing it. It's been such a long twenty-four hours since the accident. And seeing you two . . . about her age . . . It's going to be a long road back."

She reached out her arms, and I gave her my biggest, best hug for a long time, rubbing her back the way my mom does with me and my brothers when we're sad. Finally, she pulled away and found a tissue and blew her nose. "I'm so sorry! Weeping on a stranger's shoulder, on a little girl! I'm completely losing it!"

"It's totally okay. Listen, we understand. We're sorry for what happened to Angela. . . ."

"She's such a pretty girl, too," said the woman, fumbling to show us a photo on her phone.

The image came up, and we saw that the girl was truly beautiful.

"Wow," I said. "Gorgeous."

"So beautiful," agreed Olivia.

The woman clicked the phone off and put it away.

We were all quiet for a minute, looking at Angela sleeping soundly in the bed.

Then, impulsively, I pulled out my cell and showed the woman my football nose selfie. "Um, I don't know if this will make you feel better or not but . . . kids heal pretty quick. This was me a week ago." I held out the phone, and she looked at the photo, her eyes growing large and her jaw dropping.

"Really?" She looked between the photo and me, back and forth, like it didn't add up.

I smiled. "Much better, right?"

"Much." She smiled.

"Arnica cream, tea bag compresses, and parsley paste," I said with a grin and shrug. "Worked like charms."

"I'll do it," she said. "Besides all the medicine she's getting, that natural stuff could only help. Thank you."

I shrugged again. "It's amazing what time and Mother Nature can accomplish together," I said, thinking of Katie's mom.

Angela stirred in her bed, and the woman went to her side. "Honey, there are some nice girls here with cupcakes. I'll save one for when you're ready, okay?"

"Well, we'd better . . . ," I started to say.

There was a tapping on the door, and a nurse pushed it open, stopping in surprise when she saw us. "No visitors yet for Miss Angela, please!" she said firmly.

"No, it's fine. . . ." interjected Angela's mom.

"We're not visitors. . . ." I said, starting to explain.

"They're angels," said Angela's mom with a smile.

I smiled back at her.

Then I took Olivia by the arm, my cupcake carrier in my other hand, and we headed out. I called a soft good-bye over my shoulder. I got Olivia down the hall and around the corner and then found her a bench to sit on for a minute. She was clutching the snowman napkins in a death grip. I pried them from her fingers and set them on the bench next to her. Then I opened the carrier and took out a cupcake, peeling off the wrapper.

"Here, Olivia," I said. "Emergency cupcake medicine."

She took it, in a daze, and ate it, and she slowly came back to life. "I . . . don't think we were supposed to go in there," she said.

I looked at my list. "Yeah, Angela was definitely not on my list," I confirmed. "It obviously just happened, whatever it was. That poor girl. Her poor mother."

"I almost fainted," said Olivia. "The blood . . ."

"I know. Let's not talk about it. Just think happy thoughts and know that she'll be okay. A few scars, maybe, but only along the edge of her face. And at least she's alive, and she seems to have a really good mom."

Olivia nodded. "I think I want to go home," she said in a small voice.

"Okay," I agreed. We headed back to the play-room, walking quietly, lost in our own thoughts.

CHAPTER 11

Brainstorm

$\mathscr{B}$ack at the playroom, the party was wrapping up. Alexis, Mia, and Katie were thrilled by how it had all gone, chattering a mile a minute, but they stopped when they saw us.

"What happened?" asked Mia, her face full of concern.

Quietly, I explained what we had seen, and they all shook their heads sadly.

"That's so sad," Katie said, her eyes welling up.

"I know," I said with a sigh.

Kathy came bustling over and said, "Oh, my dears, I just heard from the nursing station that you got off track. Totally my fault. I'm so sorry. I should have sent someone with you. That poor child, Angela."

"What happened to her, if you don't mind my

asking?" I said. I wasn't really expecting an answer, but Kathy gave me one.

"Car accident. It wasn't her driver's fault, but Angela wasn't wearing a seat belt, so it was way worse that it should have been. She's lucky to be alive."

"Yikes," I said.

"No kidding," agreed Kathy. "You wouldn't believe how often we see it. It's a shame."

"And at this time of year," Alexis added, shaking her head sadly.

"Well, you can look at it the other way too," said Mia. "At this time of year, it's lucky she's alive. A holiday miracle."

"We have lots of those here!" Kathy said proudly. "And Angela will be fine. I promise."

We helped Kathy and her staff clean up, and we gathered our things to head downstairs. I had texted my mom to come get us, so we decided we'd just go wait outside for her. Walking out, we ran into Alexandra's dad, who was so friendly and grateful again, and we waved at some other parents who were getting ice from the machine in the hall. All in all, it was a cheerful place, with recoveries around every corner.

But Olivia had been pale and quiet ever since we'd been in Angela's room. Outside the main entrance, the cold air and the sight of the pretty snow seemed to revive her a bit more than the cupcake had, but she still looked a little upset.

"Are you all right?" I asked quietly.

"Yeah," she said, taking in deep breaths of fresh air. "It just caught me off guard. Her swollen face. And all the stitches. And ... all I could think was ... if that ever happened to me ... I don't think my mom would be so nice about it."

"Olivia! Don't be ridiculous!" I said. "Your mother would be at your side every minute!"

"I don't know. I think ... if I wasn't pretty anymore ... and part of it was my fault for not wearing a seat belt ... well ..."

I didn't like where she was going with this because part of me actually thought she might be right.

"Don't worry. We'd come cheer you up!" I said brightly, to change the tone of the conversation.

"Who?" Olivia asked distractedly.

"Us!" I said. "Your friends!"

She looked at me in surprise. "You would?"

I punched her lightly in the arm as my mom (thankfully) pulled up. "Of course!" I said, and I started toward the minivan.

"Emma!" called Olivia.

I turned back, and she was still standing there.

"Thanks," she said. And she smiled.

"You're welcome," I said. "Now hurry up and get in the car with me. It's freezing out here!"

I noticed everyone buckled up quickly as soon as we got in the car. I filled my mom in on everything, without going into too much detail about Angela other than to say it was sad. I didn't think Olivia would stand it if we dwelled too much on the subject.

We dropped off the Cupcakers at their respective houses, and as the route had it, Olivia and I were alone in the car by the end. My dad called, and my mom started talking to him on the speakerphone about dinner.

Olivia said quietly, "Emma."

"Hmm?" I turned to look at her.

"I'm sorry if I wasn't nice about your nose."

"Oh." I didn't know what to say. "Well . . . you weren't. Or maybe you were trying to be, but you just didn't know how, or whatever. It's okay."

"Well, I really am sorry," said Olivia.

"Thanks. Apology accepted," I said. I held out a hand for her to shake, and she shook it, grinning.

"You were really good with all those kids today," I said admiringly.

"Ugh. Not all of them, obviously." She grimaced.

"But, Olivia, we weren't even supposed to be in there. Even Angela's mom couldn't deal with it. Come on. All the other kids—You were so cheerful and upbeat, and you were so smart to bring the ribbons and rubber bands and the mirror! I never would have thought of that!"

"You were really good with Angela's mom," she said. "Really good. Even though I know you hate blood too."

"Well, someone had to be. We couldn't both freeze!"

"Still," she said, "I was impressed."

"Thanks," I said.

"Okay, girls, here we are!" called my mom, pulling into the Allens' driveway.

"Thanks, Mrs. Taylor," said Olivia, climbing out.

"My pleasure. Anytime!"

"Bye, Olivia!" I called. "See you at school tomorrow!"

"Bye! Thanks for including me!" She waved, and I slid the door shut.

"What a busy weekend all you girls have had!" observed my mom.

I yawned. "No kidding. All I want to do is lounge on my bed until dinner!"

"Sounds like a plan, as long as your homework is done," agreed my mom.

"It is."

Back home, I wearily climbed the stairs, looking forward to sinking onto my bed. But from Matt's room came grunts and groans of frustration.

"Matt?" I called, taking a detour toward the room he and Sam shared.

"What?" he called, all grumpy.

I pushed open his door. He was at his desk; the large screen for his computer that he'd bought himself at a yard sale had tons of windows opened on it.

"What's up?" I asked.

Matt sighed heavily and spun himself around in his desk chair to face me. "My website is driving me crazy." Matt runs a small graphic design business; he makes flyers for kids' bands, and handouts for things like dog-walking businesses (mine!), and business cards for people.

"Why?"

"I can't figure out how to add e-commerce to it, so people can pay with a credit card online or use PayPal. I watched a YouTube video on it, but there's something I'm missing."

"Why don't you go down to the computer lab at the mall? Can't they help you and maybe jazz up the site a little?"

"Nah, they'll charge me," said Matt in a defeatist tone.

"Well, I'll see if I can think of something," I said. I was no computer programmer, that was for sure. "Sorry. Good luck."

I went to my room and spied my flute case. I'd neglected practicing all weekend since I'd been so busy. It was just the thing I needed right now— relaxing and satisfying! I pulled out my flute and started practicing the pieces I'd been working on with my flute teacher, and a new one we were doing with the school orchestra.

After a while, I got bored and started just noodling around, kind of composing something. I thought of Angela today and how lucky I'd been with my injury, especially compared to hers. Seeing those sick kids today—it really put things in perspective. A bruised nose was nothing compared to what those kids were dealing with. Imagine being in a car wreck. Imagine breaking your leg and having to be in traction for eight weeks, especially if you're an athlete. Imagine having to sleep in a tent because you can't breathe. I was so lucky. And so were all my friends and family. I was glad to be reminded of it again this early in the holiday season.

My thoughts continued to roam as I played, thinking about the holiday boutique and the sleepover and the blizzard. My mom had been right. It *had* been a superbusy weekend, and I still had to figure out what to get everyone else for the holidays.

Suddenly, I thought: Why not compose a song for my friends on my flute? It wasn't a knitted hat or a beaded necklace, but it was creative, and better yet, it was free. It would last forever, and it would certainly be unique. And maybe I could even play it for Matt to use on his website!

Energized, I got out my lined music notebook and began scribbling; an hour flew by as I tried different compositions and variations, all repeating back to the same theme. I tinkered and toyed with it, and by the time my mom called us for dinner, I had something definite, though not close to finished, down on paper, and I was so psyched! I'd tried to capture Alexis's logic, Mia's flair for the dramatic and her style, and Katie's homespun simplicity and beauty. And what the heck, I even threw in a little of Olivia's surprising poise and tenderness at the hospital. I felt very proud and creatively satisfied as

I descended the stairs to dinner. I sat down at the table and Matt was smiling at me.

"I liked what you were working on," he said. "What is it?"

"Funny you should mention it!" I laughed, still all energized from my session. "It's a song I'm composing for my friends. But I wondered if you might like to use it as a soundtrack on your website?"

Matt's jaw dropped. "That's a great idea! That would really make the site come to life! Are you serious?"

I nodded, smiling, and saw that my parents were beaming at the two of us. That made me kind of roll my eyes. I hate when they get all sappy like that about our family. It's such a TV show moment.

After dinner, I dashed upstairs and texted my friends.

Homemade gifts only this year. No spending big bucks, okay? Too late?

Quickly, the replies flooded in.

GOOD CALL! said Mia.

INTO IT! wrote Katie.

And Totally, replied Alexis.

THANKS! I wrote, and I pressed send with a big grin on my face.

CHAPTER 12

Happy Holidays

The Allens' holiday party was not at all what I expected.

First of all, their house is really warm and welcoming. It made me wonder why we'd never been over there before. Mrs. Allen had gone all out with the decorations, including outdoors, and every surface was gilded or scented or ribboned or flocked. I couldn't imagine how long it would take to take it all down after the holidays.

And the food! There were platters of ham biscuits, filet of beef on crostini, apple strudel, mini pots of seafood bisque, mini-pizzas and hot dogs, croquettes, cheeses, nuts, any kind of fruit you could think of—you name it. And the dessert room was insane! A whole hallway set up with folding tables covered in pretty tablecloths bore every holiday sweet in the world: Yule logs, beautifully painted holiday cookies, brownies, candies, and hand-dipped chocolates. Best of all, there was a chocolate fondue fountain with lots of treats to dip, like marshmallows, sugar cookies, strawberries, and bananas.

We ate and ate and then made our way to the playroom, where long tables were set up for people to do holiday crafts. The cool thing was it wasn't just the kids doing it but adults, too! There were little jars to make holiday terrariums, with a selection of evergreens, and tiny reindeer and elves to use, and chubby corks to close it all up. There were picture frames you could bedazzle with jewels, and mosaic stickers that looked totally professional. Wooden dreidels sat on little stands, so you could paint them with enamel paint. And there was a section for making your own Christmas stocking or wooden clog for Santa to fill on Christmas morning. It was so fun.

Best of all, out in the garage, they'd taken out the cars, and a photographer had set up an old-time photo shoot, where you could put on costumes, have your picture taken, and get a sepia-colored print of it. We decided to do it, but Mia suggested grabbing Olivia, too, so we waited on line and then got all dressed in these wacky hats and wigs and dresses and posed really serious and unsmiling for the photo. When it came out, it was hilarious. We really looked like old-time people!

Olivia bustled around the party, actually relaxed and having fun, and her mom seemed to be in good spirits. It turned out Olivia's dad was really nice, and I guess he set the tone for the party, because he was superfriendly and a really good host, chatting with all of us, making sure we had places to leave our coats and that we got enough to eat and drink. It made me see that maybe Olivia's mom and dad represented the two sides of her—the nice and the not-as-nice. I just hoped she'd grow up to be more like her dad, even if for her own sake.

By the end of the night, we were flopped on the floor in Olivia's room, looking at photos on her laptop, talking about past holidays and laughing about what dorks we were when we were little and all the things we used to ask for the holidays.

"I was soooo into Barbies!" admitted Olivia.

"Shocker!" I laughed.

"I always liked American Girl," said Alexis.

"Me too," agreed Katie. "Especially all that furniture."

"I was more of an animal person. I think I used to get pumped for Beanie Babies, all those little kitties and puppies and stuff," I offered.

"I liked the Bratz, of course," said Mia.

"Of course!" We all laughed again. Even though we didn't know her way back when, we could be sure Mia had always been into fashion.

"What are you guys asking for this year?" asked Olivia.

Everyone mentioned a thing or two, but we agreed there was nothing anyone really wanted. "I'm doing a lot of homemade gifts this year," I said.

"That's such a good idea!" said Olivia. "Maybe I'll do that. I've still got a week."

I couldn't believe this was the same Olivia Allen I'd wanted to punch in the nose only a few days earlier. It's amazing what the holiday spirit will do to people—to her and to me, of course.

"Well, I think we'd better get going," I said, standing up. "Olivia, this was one of the best parties I've ever been to in my life. And I'm not just saying that. Thank you so much."

"Thank you all for coming," she said. "This really . . . meant a lot to me. It's the best present I could have gotten this year," she added shyly.

We thanked her parents and got our coats, and

Olivia walked us to the door and hugged everyone good-bye. None of us said anything, but I knew we were feeling guilty. My dad was picking us up so that everyone could come sleep over at my house and exchange gifts. I toyed with the idea of spontaneously inviting Olivia, but I knew it would be awkward since no one had a gift for her. We could be friends with her, but she wasn't a member of the Cupcake Club. At least not for the foreseeable future.

Back at my house, my brothers were all there, and some of their friends too, and it turned out to be kind of a rowdy and fun end of the night. We played Ping-Pong in the basement, and mini-hockey on the rug in the TV room, and then we watched *A Christmas Story* on TV and had popcorn. I suddenly had the idea that Alexis could help Matt with his website as a holiday gift, and she thought that was brilliant. She vowed to go home and create a gift certificate to present to him this week. Later, the Cupcakers and I trudged upstairs to my room to lay out the sleeping bags and exchange our gifts.

Mia went first. She'd designed stretchy headbands for all of us, and her mom's friend had run them up on a sewing machine. They were so perfect. Alexis's was navy blue velvet with seed pearls, and it looked so pretty against her red hair. Katie's was purple with multicolored sequins sewn on, and mine was white satin with a lace overlay to wear at Mona's for my next job. It was so thoughtful.

Katie had loomed each of us an elaborate-colored rubber band bracelet. Mine was an elaborate rainbow heart, and I couldn't imagine how long it had taken her to make it. Alexis's was a star pattern, and Mia's was a square pattern, chunky, like something a model would wear. They all looked awesome and so stylish.

Alexis went next and she handed around date books for each of us. She'd covered them with pretty contact paper in different patterns for each of us, and then she'd filled in important dates inside that corresponded to our interests. Katie's had NYC Restaurant Week blocked out and her favorite chefs' birthdays marked with big stars. Mia's had Fashion Week blocked out, as well as the Oscars and a bunch of her favorite fashion designers' birthdays highlighted. Mine had listings of my favorite composers' birthdays, as well as having the New York Philharmonic's main concert dates penciled in. It was so thoughtful.

And, finally, it was my turn.

I stood and cleared my throat.

"Uh-oh!" joked Mia.

"A speech!" said Alexis.

"No, it's a poem!" Katie laughed.

"Actually," I said, fake-glaring at them, "I have composed a song for you. It has Alexis's logic and organization, Mia's passion and drama, and Katie's beauty and comfort. I'll play it now and then make a recording to send to you by e-mail."

I opened my flute case, so I didn't have to meet anyone's eye. I hoped they weren't laughing at me. I'd worked so hard on it, but part of me thought it might be a lame gift, or a cop-out, now that it was actually time to perform it. But it was all that I had. Just a part of me to give to them.

I cleared my throat, licked my lips, and raised the flute to my mouth. Then I closed my eyes and began to play. It seemed to last forever, but when it was over, I was scared to open my eyes. There was a dead silence, and finally, I opened my eyes and looked at my friends.

They were all crying.

I started to laugh and cry at the same time. "Did you like it?"

Mia laughed and wiped at her eyes. "Like it? Silly, we *loved* it!"

They grabbed me and pulled me into a big group hug.

"That's the best present I've even gotten, and I am not kidding. Even better than my Felicity doll from American Girl!" said Katie, and we all laughed.

"Well, it wasn't better than an Easy-Bake oven, but it was pretty close," joked Alexis. "It was just beautiful."

They squeezed me tightly, and I knew that nothing was more beautiful than friendship. Especially during the holidays.

Want another sweet cupcake?

Here's a sneak peek

of the next book in the

CUPCAKE 🧁 DIARIES

series:

Alexis's

cupcake

cupid

Table 4 Two

$\mathcal{P}$ink sparkly sugar?"

Katie peered into her shopping basket. "Check."

"Red food coloring?" I continued.

"Check."

"Heart-shaped Red Hots?"

"Check."

"Red-and-white–striped cupcake wrappers?"

"Check."

"Red gel frosting?"

"Check."

"Yay! Time to check out!" I said cheerfully.

I led the way to the register at Baker's Hollow, the baking supplies store at the mall, and the Cupcake Club's home away from home. We had just been asked by a friend of Emma's mom—somewhat last minute—to bake two dozen cupcakes for a ladies' Valentine's Day luncheon tomorrow.

Today is Saturday and the real Valentine's Day is Monday, so we had decided to shop for the supplies together, just for fun. Since I run the finances for our baking club (with the other members' skills as follows: Mia is in charge of style and appearance, Emma is in charge of marketing and publicity, and Katie is in charge of recipes), I had the money and was in charge of paying and then logging the purchase into my newly automated Excel spreadsheet on my tablet. (It replaced my leatherbound accounts ledger, which was running out of pages.)

The plan today was to get supplies for our Valentine's cupcakes, buy Valentine's Day cards for our families, then head back to Emma's to whip up cupcakes and *then*, maybe a sleepover. But first we needed lunch.

In the food court, a new Asian street-food place had just opened, and we had to check it out. Emma loves spicy Asian food, and so does Mia. Katie likes all types of cuisines, and I don't like spicy food at all, but Emma and Mia begged us, so we agreed to try it. The menu was awesome, and it had so many choices: dumplings, both steamed and pan-fried; marinated skewers of chicken and beef; scallion pancakes loaded with barbecue pork; noodles with shrimp and mushrooms, and every kind of topping you could imagine!

I was studying the menu when Mia interrupted my thoughts. "Hey! I heard that the theme for the middle-school Family Skating Party this year is Chinese New Year! Won't that be cool?"

I am dreading the Family Skating Party more than maybe I have ever dreaded anything. Clearly, I am alone in this.

"Awesome!" Katie agreed with Mia. "They could do such pretty red party decor with that theme, and it kind of ties in with Valentine's Day."

"Great food options with the Chinese theme, too. Much better than the Wild West theme last year," said Emma. "I hate eating ribs in public. So messy." She shook her head and laughed.

The other girls laughed too, and I imagined chasing the butterflies in my stomach around with a net and then whacking them!

"Alexis, is something wrong? You're being very quiet," Mia said.

"Yes," I answered grimly. "But don't you remember that I can't skate?"

"Wait, I thought you were going to take lessons!" said Emma.

I shook my head. "Didn't have time. I still stink. I think I might not go." I hated to miss a social opportunity where I might get to interact "in the real world" with Matt Taylor, Emma's brother and the crush of my life. But that was the primary reason I *wasn't* going. I couldn't stand the idea of being mortified in front of Matt. What if he saw that I was a bad skater? He's such a jock—he'd totally lose respect for me.

"Wait, *whaaaat*? What do you mean you might not go? You have to go!" said Emma, just as we reached the front of the line.

"I don't want to discuss it," I said. "Let's order."

We pooled our money and ordered a bunch of different stuff to mix and match and share. The place was really busy, and it only had these long communal tables, so while we waited for our food to be ready, we split up and got busy scouting for people who were leaving.

Katie found a very tight spot for us after a few minutes, and Mia and Emma went to help save the seats while I returned to the counter to wait for our order. I saw my friend Ella Klinsky from school, and we waved and gestured to how crazy-busy the place was. Now that I was looking around, I could see that a lot of kids from school were here, sprinkled around. This Asian restaurant was popular with middle schoolers, that was for sure. I wondered how many of them could skate.

I was lost in thought, holding the little buzzer that they give you to tell you when your food is ready, twirling it in my hands and thinking about Valentine's Day. I know I am the no-nonsense type, but I am also kind of a sucker for all that romance stuff, believe it or not. I love the love songs on the radio, the romantic shows on TV, and my mom always decorates the table on Valentine's Day morning for breakfast. We have heart-shaped pancakes, and she gives us cards and candy and a little pink or red present, like cute red socks or something. It's a fun way to spice up blah old February, and I was looking forward to it.

Suddenly, someone right close behind me said, "Lexi?" I jumped and whirled around.

"Matt!" I cried. It was Matt Taylor, in the flesh! "Hi!" I felt myself blush hard (speaking of something red!), but I couldn't stop grinning.

"Hi!" he said, laughing. "Did I scare you?"

"Well, I don't exactly expect people to sneak up behind me in places like this and then speak directly into my ear!" I said, as if I was annoyed, but really I was just the opposite—thrilled!

"Sorry." He smiled, kind of shy. "Uh, what do you recommend here?"

I looked up at the menu, still smiling like a dope. "Well, we got . . ." And as I started to list our order, my buzzer went off, and I jumped again.

Matt was really laughing at me now. "A little jumpy today, are we?"

"Hungry, maybe!" I said. I handed my buzzer to the girl at the counter, and she handed me our tray. I looked down at it, and my mouth began to water. My friends were waiting, my food was ready, but I didn't want to leave. "Uh . . . where are you sitting?" I asked.

"I haven't found a spot yet. I'm solo. I'm sure I can just wedge in somewhere," he said, all casual. It was almost his turn to order.

"Well . . . join us if you want. We can squeeze together," I said, wincing inwardly. Our spot was tiny. But I would happily squeeze in for him.

"Thanks. I'll look for you after I get my food."

I said good-bye and went to my friends, lowering the heavy tray onto the table. "Hey, Em, Matt's here," I said, like it was totally normal and cool.

She glanced up. "Oh yeah? He said he needed to go to the sporting goods store today, so I'm not surprised."

"He has no one to eat with," I said, doling out the food and perching on the end of the bench.

"Well, he can't sit here," Emma said grumpily. "There's no room!"

I grimaced and took a bite of a dumpling. It was delicious, and for a few minutes of bliss, I forgot all about Matt and ice-skating. "This is insane! Sooooo yummy!" I moaned.

We all traded containers and bites back and forth. Then I remembered about Matt, and I looked around. He had found a seat on his own near the end of another table. His back was to us and the seat across from him was empty. My heart clenched a little to see him eating all alone. I wanted to go join him, but I was nervous that my friends would get mad if I ditched them. Or worse, that if I went over there, someone would sit in the empty seat just as I reached it, and I'd be left standing there like a nerd—that would be so embarrassing. My palms began to sweat a little as I wrestled with the decision. *Should I stay or should I go?* I'd lost my appetite.

The other girls began discussing what they were going to get at the stationery store, and I sort of followed along distractedly as I stared at Matt's strong back and broad shoulders. I wondered if I should give him a valentine this year. The very thought made me feel sick to my stomach, but my dad always said you should do what you are afraid of doing, so maybe I should do it. Hmm.

"Okay, Alexis?" asked Emma.

"Huh? What?" I said, snapping out of my day-dream.

"The stationery store?"

"Oh. Uh . . . you know what? I'll just meet you there in a few minutes, okay? I . . . have one more thing to do." Did I really just ditch my friends for a boy? *Bad, bad Alexis!* But if they caught on, they didn't seem to mind, and they didn't ask any questions (and I didn't offer any further explanation). We threw out our garbage—sorting everything into three cool-looking bins—one for food waste, one for paper stuff (which was most of it), and one for the few plastic cups and forks. Then they headed off and I doubled back to Matt's table. Luckily, Matt had bought a lot of food, so he was only about two thirds of the way finished.

"Hey," I said, all casual.

"Hey! Sit down!" He smiled and then wiped his mouth. "Awesome food, right?"

"Awesome," I agreed, perching in the mercifully still-empty seat across from him. "It was definitely time for a change around here. They needed to mix it up. I mean, how much Chinese food and pizza can they expect us to eat?"

Matt laughed and put his hand over his heart. "Hey, don't bust on my Panda Gardens."

I glanced across the food court at the Panda Gardens counter where everything was quiet. "You'd better get some soon, because I don't think they're going to be here much longer."

Matt gasped, all fake-horrified. "Take it back!"

I laughed. "I won't!" I put my hands to my mouth, like I was going to yell over to Panda Gardens, *Hey, PG, time to pack it in!*

Matt reached for my hands and tried to pry them from my face. I was laughing, and he was laughing, and I kept putting up my hands, so he would keep grabbing them away. It was funny, and it was soooo nice to feel his hands touch mine. He held my hands for one instant extra. We were both smiling, and then he said, "Well, I don't want to keep you from your friends."

"Oh, that's okay. They're in the stationery store. I have to go meet them in a minute. What are you up to now?"

Matt told me his errand list as we stood up together and went to recycle or throw away his stuff. We found ourselves at the edge of the seating area, about to part ways. I was desperate to think of a way to prolong the encounter or to get him to touch my hands again, but I was distracted by his cuteness. My brain just wasn't working fast enough.

"So maybe I'll see you later?" I asked. "We're baking at your house today."

"Oh, cool. Okay. I'll be back after my practice. My dad is taking me straight from here, so . . ." It actually seemed like he wasn't ready to part yet either, which made me really psyched.

"Well . . ." I stalled.

He grabbed my hand and gave it a squeeze. "Lay off Panda Gardens!" he said with a smile, and then he quickly dropped my hand and walked away without looking back.

I stood there grinning like an idiot. Then I whispered, "Thank you, Panda Gardens!" Promising myself to eat there sometime soon, I went to find my friends.

Be Mine

$\mathcal{A}t$ the stationery store, the other girls were in valentine heaven. Katie had gathered supplies to make homemade valentines—paper doilies, glitter, glue, and pink and red construction paper. Mia had an assortment of stuff she was going to use to make crafty little gifts—small white cardboard boxes to decorate with sticker gems and then fill with little candies. Emma had selected a fat stack of ready-made valentines.

I was still all googly-eyed over Matt, but I didn't want to be weird about it around Emma, so I stayed off to the side and busied myself with the cards. I selected some regular ones for my parents and my older sister, Dylan, and then I continued my silent debate about buying one for Matt. I edged away from the family cards section ("For a wonderful Mother on Valentine's Day!") and into the funny greeting card area. I looked around to see if my friends were watching (they weren't), and then I quickly started rifling through the card selection, looking for one I might be able to give to Matt. They were all funny, but some were too forward, some assumed too much; many were way too lovey-dovey. I didn't know what to do!

What I needed was a card that said something like, "Hey, crush! I really like you, but if you don't like me like that, then pretend you never got this card. Oh, and don't tell anyone, either. Especially your sister, who is my best friend!"

Ha. Guess how many cards like that I found?

Sighing heavily, I circled up to the counter to pay for my three measly cards.

Mia sidled up next to me with her stuff. "All set?" she asked.

"I guess," I said. I glanced around to see where Emma, was and when I saw she was far across the store, I added, "I wanted to get something for Matt, but nothing here is really right."

Mia nodded in understanding. "Could you make him a valentine?"

I grimaced. "That seems so . . . serious. Like, a

lot of effort to put in, and what if he doesn't like me like that?"

Mia rolled her eyes and smiled. "Oh, I think he likes you like that. I wouldn't worry about it!"

"Really?" I couldn't hold back the huge grin that burst onto my face. "So maybe I should get him a card?"

Mia frowned thoughtfully. "Well . . . maybe it's better not to put anything in writing just yet. You know?"

It was now my turn to pay. I stepped forward. "So should I go back and get him some little gift?"

Mia furrowed her brow as she debated it.

"Next?" the lady at the counter called, a little annoyed. I had to pay.

I put down my stuff on the counter, and Mia was called to the register next to me.

She continued, "Why don't you get him something small . . . like, hmm. Flowers are too girlie. Too serious, anyway. Maybe a teddy bear?"

I shook my head. "Also a little girlie, I think?"

"Hey! Why don't you say it with cupcakes?" Mia suggested brightly. "You already know he loves cupcakes!"

"Who loves cupcakes?" said Katie, coming up behind us.

"Matt," I whispered.

Katie smiled. "Are you thinking of your valentine?"

I felt myself blush yet again. "Maybe," I said, turning to pay.

"How was your date?" asked Katie.

I whipped my head around. "What date?"

Katie was grinning. "Lunch at the mall?"

Busted!

"That wasn't a date! That was just . . . me not liking to see a friend eat alone." I shrugged, all casual, and took my bag from the cashier.

"Riiiiight!" Katie laughed. "That's why you didn't tell us where you were going!"

"It was a daaaaate!" singsonged Mia.

"Oh, shush!" I said, fake-annoyed but kind of pleased, too.

"Are you getting him something?" asked Katie.

"Well . . . I'm just debating. What do you think?" I asked, kind of hoping she'd say yes.

"Um, I don't know. Maybe wait and see if he gets *you* something?"

Oh.

Just then Emma arrived. "What's up? How did Matt like the new restaurant?"

"Oh, gosh. I'm sorry. I just . . ."

Emma smiled. "It's okay. You can be honest with us, though. You don't need to hide that you want to hang out with him. I'll let you know if it's cutting into our girl time," she said with a playful nudge.

I smiled goofily. "Thanks."

"Did you get him a card?" asked Emma, peering at my bag. She dumped her stuff on the counter and took out her wallet.

"No," I said.

"Good," Emma said, nodding firmly. "He's not really the mushy type."

O-kaaaay! I thought. *Now you tell me!*

"But Alexis *should* get him something, I think," protested Mia. "Or at least bake something for him. Maybe a bunch of cupcakes arranged on a platter into the shape of a heart?"

I winced. "That's a little psycho looking, I think."

"Food's not a bad idea," Emma agreed, taking her bag from the cashier. We headed to the exit. I felt myself hanging on her every word, like she was the expert on the subject of Matt Taylor.

"Like, what kind of food? Chocolates?" I asked eagerly.

"Nah." Emma shook her head. "He's not crazy about chocolate."

"Gummy worms?" I asked.

Emma smiled. "Do gummy worms really say romance?"

"True. What about cupcakes?"

Maybe Mia's idea wasn't so boring.

"Maybe . . . ," said Emma.

Suddenly, I felt a little annoyed. Like, why did Emma get all the power to decide what I should get Matt? He was only her brother. It wasn't like she knew him as a boyfriend or whatever. And why would Katie discourage me from doing something? Was she jealous because she and George Martinez are kind of on-and-off? Or did she really think I shouldn't get Matt something first, like I was being too pushy? Then again, maybe I should take Mia's advice and do something romantic, really let him know I like him like *that*.

There were so many options! So many decisions! So many ways . . . to embarrass myself. I felt aggravated now.

"You know what? Thanks, everyone. I'll figure something out," I said, more cheerfully than I felt. My brain was swirling with ideas and opinions, and I was a little sick of discussing it. Valentines by committee are probably not a good idea.

"My only advice for you is: less is more," said Emma.

I huffed. "Thanks," I said. *Sort of,* I added in my mind.

Mia threw me a sympathetic glance. "Hey," she said. "At least you like someone! I feel like I don't even know any boys!"

"Me, neither!" Katie agreed, at which point we all had to tease her about George.

"And I know too many!" Emma cried, who was always sick of living in boyland at her house.

"Poor Emma," said Mia, fake sympathetic.

We all laughed and then went out to meet Emma's mom for a ride home.

Back at the Taylors', I pulled my tablet from out of my bag and ducked into the bathroom, where I sat on the lid of the toilet and made a small list of the pros and cons of giving Matt a valentine of any sort.

Pros:
It would be nice of me.
He would probably like it.
Maybe it would take things to the next
     level.
Maybe he would give me something.
Maybe he would ask me out on a date.

Cons:
What if he doesn't like me like that?
What if Emma gets annoyed?
I am scared to go on a date.
What if he doesn't give me anything back?
What if he doesn't like what I give him?

I stared at the list. Yes or no? Do or die? Do *and* die (of embarrassment!)?

"Alexis?"

It was Emma calling me.

"In here!" I replied through the closed door.

"You okay? It's time to start baking!" she called.

"Coming!" I called, scrambling to tuck my tablet back in its sleeve.

I decided right then. One cupcake. That's all. That's what I'd give him. He could take it any way he wanted. One little cupcake. How much trouble could that be?

Want more

cupcake Diaries?

Visit **CupcakeDiariesBooks.com**
for the series trailer, excerpts, activities,
and everything you need for throwing
your own cupcake party!

Coco Simon always dreamed of opening a cupcake bakery but was afraid she would eat all of the profits. When she's not daydreaming about cupcakes, Coco edits children's books and has written close to one hundred books for children, tweens, and young adults, which is a lot less than the number of cupcakes she's eaten. Cupcake Diaries is the first time Coco has mixed her love of cupcakes with writing.

Looking for another great book?
Find it in the middle.

in
the
middle
BOOKS

Fun, fantastic books for kids
in the in-beTWEEN age.

IntheMiddleBooks.com

If you liked

CUPCAKE  DIARIES

be sure to check out these

other series from

Simon Spotlight

IT TAKES TWO

If you like reading about the adventures of Katie, Mia, Emma, and Alexis, you'll love Alex and Ava, stars of the It Takes Two series!

EBOOK EDITIONS ALSO AVAILABLE
ItTakesTwoBooks.com • Published by Simon Spotlight • Kids.SimonandSchuster.com

sew zoey

Zoey's clothing design blog
puts her on the A-list in the
fashion world . . . but when
it comes to school, will she
be teased, or will she be a
trendsetter? Find out in the
Sew Zoey series:

EBOOK EDITIONS ALSO AVAILABLE
SewZoeyBooks.com • Published by Simon Spotlight • Kids.SimonandSchuster.com